AN Angel FOR Christmas

HEATHER GRAHAM

AN *Angel* FOR *Christmas*

MIRA®

ISBN-13: 978-0-7783-1279-6

AN ANGEL FOR CHRISTMAS

www.MIRABooks.com

Printed in U.S.A.

First Printing: October 2011
10 9 8 7 6 5 4 3 2 1

To Eric Curtis
Certainly one of the world's finest photographers

Prologue

Gabe Lange's quarry was right in front of him.

The chase had begun in vehicles, his a police cruiser. The perp had quickly taken the lead in a stolen Maserati. Still, Gabe had discovered that the police car was well equipped to handle such a race, and he'd been right behind him all the way. In fact, while the con had eventually crashed into a snowbank, he'd managed to swerve to a stop, without even spinning in the snow and ice as he might have done.

Luke had surely faced some injury in the crash; sore muscles, if nothing else. Gabe had come out unscathed. But Luke appeared to be good at disappearing, even amidst a crash, and for a moment—when Gabe had followed him up the first steep hill that led to the road up the mountain—he'd lost him.

He could not lose him; it was Christmas Eve. He couldn't let Luke loose on some unsuspecting family about to settle down to a Christmas Eve dinner. He could already picture the kind of home where Luke might try to find entry; a couple placing the last of the presents under the tree, perhaps. There might be a crèche set up on a coffee table, a tree with brilliant lights facing the parlor or living room with a multipaned window allowing the lights to shine upon the snow. Little ones would be put to bed; the father might be doing the last work, scratching his head as he tried to follow the "simple" instructions for finishing a bike or a video system that would be there, big and beautiful, beneath the tree. Here, especially here, in the mountains of Virginia, people had a habit of being welcoming. The houses and old cabins were few and far between, and the neighbors, even those who only came for the summer and holidays, learned to be welcoming and giving. Usually, of course.

Maybe Luke would happen upon the one family who was more than wary of strangers, and ready with a shotgun.

But Gabe hadn't lost Luke; when he came around a copse of trees, he saw him again, limping, but continuing upward once again. The roads here were poorly plowed, but even with snowdrifts swirling through the air and the few feet of accumulation, the path that led to the sparse population here was apparent; it was an indentation in the banks of snow.

And Luke was heading toward it.

Gabe quickened his pace, grateful that he had the kind of body that had been kept in shape; powerful arms and legs, and good lungs. That seemed especially important now. Breathing was good one minute—the air being so crisp, smogless, empty of diesel fuel, the fumes of buses and trucks—and then hard the next; the snow was still coming.

He heard his own breathing as he surged on upward. Luke had a body that was honed as well; young, muscled and lithe. Had he been a gymnast or a sprinter at some time? He was moving just like—just like a bat out of hell.

Huffing and puffing, Gabe kept climbing. When he reached the road, Luke had once again disappeared.

He held very still, trying to listen.

But the snow kept the dried branches of the naked, skeletal trees snapping and the wind that hurried the snow flurries along seemed to whistle and moan; he couldn't hear any other sound.

He turned, searching out the trees, and then he looked to his feet, hoping that the flurries weren't falling fast enough to erase all signs of footprints.

He could barely make them out. Luke had escaped across the road into the trees to the northwest, but it seemed that he'd somehow doubled back….

That realization dawned just in time for Gabe to

turn around halfway and almost ward off the blow that came his way when the perp, Luke, cracked him hard over the head with a massive oak branch. The wood was dry and brittle, and he could almost hear it cry out at the abuse as his own head began to spin, and the jarring pain took hold.

Gabe fell to his knees. Luke let out the sound of delighted laughter. "Gotcha!" he said.

No. It wasn't ending here. Gabe wasn't dying in a pile of snow while Luke went on to torment a family on Christmas Eve.

Or worse.

He reached out, glad of his strength as he snaked a firm grip around his opponent's ankle, jerking him off his feet. Luke crashed down beside him. He tried to seize the advantage and jump on his quarry, but Luke rolled, and Gabe was left to stagger to his feet. There was something trickling down his forehead, blinding him.

Blood.

He let out a cry of determination and flew at Luke, tackling him down into the snow. Luke fell once again. Gabe landed a good hook to Luke's left cheek, but he had no time for satisfaction. Luke, bellowing in pain, still managed to catch hold of something in the snow.

A rock.

"Oh, my old friend! The night is mine now. I'm ahead of you at every step!" Luke said with pleasure.

Go figure. Luke found a rock on the road beneath the snow. As proud as a crow, he held it for a fraction of a second above Gabe.

"The challenge is on—and you've lost already!" he said.

He brought the rock down hard against Gabe's skull, and Gabe went down....

He saw the flurries in the sky, and couldn't help but think, *How beautiful. So much on God's earth, even in winter, was stunningly beautiful...*

He slumped down, stars spinning before his eyes, and then fading away to the blackness of a moonless night...

Gabe came to; he didn't know how much later. He blinked away the pain, and pressed cold snow against his face, hoping that would help clear his head. It did.

He tried to stagger to his feet. His first attempt failed; he tried again.

When he stood, he realized that his vision was fine. The world seemed to be a strange shade of gray because dusk was falling. Somewhere, people were watching the extraordinary show of the sun sinking in the west; here, the day was just going from opaque and overcast to the murky gray that promised a very dark night very soon.

Which way had Luke gone?

He brought his gloved fingers to his face, and noted that something was off. He stretched out his arms and looked down at his legs, and groaned.

Luke had stolen his clothing—his Virginia Department of Law Enforcement uniform.

God help him. The challenge was really on now.

Chapter 1

The landscape was crystal, dusted in a fresh fall of snow that seemed to make tree branches shimmer, as if they were dotted with jewels.

Of course, the same new snow that made everything so beautiful could also become treacherous, Morwenna thought, trying to adjust her defroster as the car climbed up the mountainside.

With her initial reaction of, "How beautiful," barely out of her mind, she wondered why her parents hadn't decided to buy a retreat in the Bahamas, Arizona or Florida instead of forever main-taining the centuries-old, difficult-to-heat rustic old cabin in the Blue Ridge Mountains. If the snow started up again—which forecasters were predicting—the beauty would definitely become dangerous.

"Other people opt for warmth," she muttered aloud. "Birds do it—they fly south for the winter!" If the snow had started up a bit earlier, she might have had a great excuse not to come.

That thought immediately made her feel guilty. She loved her parents. She even loved her siblings—with whom she'd been fighting all her life. But this was going to be a rough Christmas. She winced; Shayne was going to be miserable. *His own fault.* She'd tried to tell her brother many times that he needed to start working harder at com-municating if he was going to save his marriage. Shayne always thought that he was doing the right thing, and, of course, if it was the *right* thing in his head, everyone knew it was the wrong thing. Then, of course, there was Bobby. Baby brother Bobby, hardly a baby anymore; he was on his third college, having come home midsemester twice. Bobby was brilliant, which made her all the more angry with him, but so far, he'd majored in political science, education and biology. Now, he was once again searching for himself.

She was about to stop the car; the flurries were growing stronger, and even in her nice little Audi, the defrosting system was beginning to wear out. But then it appeared before her. The old family "cottage" in the woods on the mountaintop. Her mother had grown up there, but Morwenna and her siblings had not. When Stacy Byrne had met the rising young attorney from Philadelphia, Michael MacDougal, she had fallen head over heels in love, and had left home behind to follow him, wherever he might lead. But she'd lost her parents at a young age, and the house had become hers. By then, of course, it had needed extensive repairs and just about a new everything to remain standing. Her father might have joined a zillion private firms as a criminal defense attorney and made oodles of money, but he liked working in the D.A.'s office, and that was where he had stayed. They had never wanted for anything, but she often felt sorry for her dad—maintaining the cottage in the mountains had precluded any possibility of him buying one of those nice little time-shares in the islands or a warmer climate.

They were all grown up now—well, more or less. Bobby was twenty-one. But every time Morwenna thought about a brilliant excuse *not* to join her family for Christmas and accept one of the invitations she so often received to head to Jamaica or Grand Cayman for the holiday, she always chickened out at the last minute. Was that actually chickening out? No! Honestly, it was doing the right thing. Maybe she was feeling an edge—even an edge of bitterness—because Alex Hampton had urged her to join him for a jaunt to Cancún for an eight-day hiatus, a lovely bout of warmth from Christmas Eve until January 2. Of course, she'd asked Alex to join her in the mountains, but others from their office were going to Cancún, and, he'd explained, he had to go since he was the one who had instigated the trip.

Sure, he'd had to go. Why? He couldn't have just

explained that the two of them were dating—no, more than dating. They were together. They should have been together at Christmas.

Well, he hadn't. And—perhaps because he'd been so stubborn, she'd been stubborn as well. And maybe she had hoped until the last minute that Alex would realize he was in love with her, and he had to come with her on a family holiday.

But he hadn't.

So Alex was on his way to Cancún, and she was...nearly blinded in the snow on top of a frigid mountain in Virginia.

She should have given in, she thought.

But he should have wanted to be with her; Christmas was a time for family!

At that moment, the cabin appeared before her. For a moment, it looked like a shack in the wilderness. Then it seemed that the snow miraculously cleared. She saw the porches, and the extensions of the wings. And from inside, the lights from a Christmas tree. Red and blue, green and yellow, festive and glittering out onto the snow. Her mother's home was reputed to have once been the property of Thomas Jefferson, or at least the property of a Jefferson-family relative. It had been a tavern way back when, and had eighteenth-century pocket doors that slid across the parlor; at night, when the family had finished with the business of the day, children had been sent upstairs to bed while the doors had been opened, and all in the vicinity came to drink—and, she'd heard, plot against the British. During the Civil War, the MacDougals had been what would have been referred to today as "closet" Abolitionists, which had made the place part of the Underground Railroad. It did have history, she thought. She was amused to think as well that, since the area was known a bit for the Hatfield-and-McCoy kind of feuding, it had even survived the aftermath of the war, when grown men had dressed up in sheets as the Klan and come around burning down those who had aided the North in any way.

"So, it's still ours!" she murmured.

She had arrived.

Morwenna wasn't sure if her other siblings had arrived yet, or how they had come, but the garage door was open despite the snow. Her mother wouldn't have wanted them to have to stop to open the doors, and the kids no longer had automatic openers for the door.

She wished that, in all their great wisdom, they'd managed a garage that connected directly to the house. But they hadn't.

She grabbed her bag and, huffing and grunting, dislodged it from her small car. She slipped out the side door and headed for the house.

Once again, she stared at it.

"You're a white elephant!" she said aloud to the structure.

Naturally, it didn't reply.

She began the trudge to the porch. "Home, yep. Oh, yeah, home for the holidays."

Bobby MacDougal added another ornament to the tree, wincing as he heard what had been the low murmur of his parents' voices grow to a pitch that was far louder.

They were fighting about him, of course. They'd

fought about him many times in his twenty-one years of life; he was the misfit of the family.

He didn't want them fighting about him. Then again, while his mother had a tendency to view the world through Pollyanna eyes, and his father was more on the doom-and-gloom side and was always practical. But, then, of course, he worked with the worst of humanity at times, and Bobby had to figure that swayed his thinking now and then. On the other side, his mother liked to believe that everything was going to be all right when there wasn't a snowball's chance in hell that it would be.

Still, he didn't want to be the cause of their argument.

He'd tried—good God, he'd tried, really— but he hated the law. His father always thought it would be great if he got a degree in anything that was academic, and he had always understood facts and figures, and he honestly loved the different sciences. But he only loved exploration as a hobby, he didn't want to dissect frogs or other cold-blooded creatures that the powers that be had decided were fine to take apart. He now knew what he wanted; he just knew that his parents would be horrified, and so, since he had arrived at the mountaintop a few days ago, he'd tried to keep silent and listen to the lectures.

And those lectures were endless.

He understood that his father was a super-achiever, but his father of all people should have understood. Mike MacDougal made a decent living; he might have swept the world away. He had chosen not to, which would make people think that he'd be understanding of the fact that his son wasn't looking to dominate the stock market, just something to do for a living that would suffice—as long as he was happy. Bobby had tried once to explain that he didn't need to make a fortune; he wanted to get along fine. He'd made the argument that when the economy went down, even computer scientists were struggling for a living, and that nurses might be in high demand, but hospitals couldn't pay them. His father always just stared at him blankly.

Bobby looked at the little ornament he held. He

hadn't realized that he'd picked it up, or what it was—one of his mom's cherished antiques. It was a little angel with a trumpet. He assumed that the angel was trumpeting the birth of Christ.

"Ah, but maybe you're just a naked little cherub—advertising!" he told the ornament.

He could really hear the voices from the kitchen now. His father's voice was growing aggravated. "Look, Stacy, you're missing the point. He's going to wind up being a bum on the streets of New York, drinking out of a paper bag and asking for handouts. And for what? Because he 'can't find himself'?"

"Shh! He'll hear you," his mother whispered.

"He should hear me—he knows how I feel. You've got Morwenna, working more than sixty hours a week at that ad firm, and you've got Shayne, who works all day *as a doctor,* and comes home to take care of the kids."

"Shayne only takes care of the kids on his day," Stacy MacDougal reminded her husband.

Mike was silent for a minute. "The point is," he said. "He works hard."

"Too hard," Stacy said more quietly.

"If that bitch of a wife of his had just appreci-ated the time he was putting in for her and the kids, she'd still be with him—and she and the kids would have been here, too," Mike said.

"I am going to miss the children terribly!" Stacy said.

At least they'd stopped talking about him! Bobby thought. *Still, he was sad. He'd cared about his sister-in-law. She had her eccentricities like everyone alive; she had probably just been fed up. Shayne was so seldom home; she had little help and no social life.*

"The thing is this—no matter what, Shayne and Morwenna are going to be all right," Mike said. "They know how to *work.* They'll survive. You know, Stacy, life isn't one big Christmas holiday. It's reality. You have to work to make a living. You have to make a living to have food and shelter!"

Back to him!

He set the angel or cherub or antique-whatever on the tree. As he did so, he heard the purr of an engine and hurried over to the window—the Audi. Morwenna had arrived.

Morwenna would jump right into the lectures with their father. Great. At least Shayne was just depressed beyond all measure, so tangled up in his own misery over his divorce that he wasn't about to pick on anyone else. He'd be able to let Shayne bemoan the loss of his wife as soon as he arrived. Better than listening to the same lecture over and over again.

"Hey!" he cried loudly. "Morwenna's here!"

Bobby hurried to the door, rushing out to help his sister with her bag. He grinned as he saw her; Morwenna was always the height of fashion. She'd grown into a stunning woman, tall and leggy, with eyes so deep a blue they were the kind referred to as violet. Her hair was their dad's pitch-black, although now, Mike MacDougal's hair was definitely showing more than minor touches of distinguished gray. Morwenna's hair, however, was the old MacDougal hair, as lustrous as a raven's wing. And stylish, of course. Perfectly coiffed. She was in advertising and marketing, and he knew that in her mind, people trusted you to make them look good when *you* looked good.

"Baby bro!" she said, dropping the suitcase to give him a fierce hug.

That's the way it always started out; hugs and kisses and warmth and happiness.

Then…drumroll…the sniping began!

"Hey, big sis," he said. He frowned, looking around. "Where's the boy toy?"

She looked at him with irritation. "*Alex* is in Cancún. He couldn't get out of it. I guess he planned it before he knew that I had to come home. He kept trying to get me to go, but…"

"Ah, poor girl! Cancún. Hmm. And he went without you," Bobby said.

"It's business, Bobby. He had others in the firm going with him."

"Sure," Bobby said.

"Let's get this inside. I can do the carrying. Was it bad getting up?"

"Horrible."

"I hope that Shayne is close behind," Bobby said.

"Hey, I'm just glad that Shayne is coming! I've talked to him, and he is just about the most depressed man in the world right now," Morwenna said, her voice troubled. "I hope he doesn't back out and work hundred-hour emergency shifts just to have something to do."

"Shayne is coming. He said he might not have the ex or his kids, but we'd be the best place a depressed lonely guy could be for Christmas," Bobby assured her.

"*Our* family is the best group to be with when you're depressed?" She laughed.

He grinned. "Family—the only people you can rip to shreds in the name of love! Naw, we'll make him feel better."

"Good. At least, I think so!" Morwenna said. She glanced at him. "Well, how's it going for you?"

"Fine."

She looked at him skeptically. "Honestly, though, Bobby, you dropped out again?"

He sighed. "I didn't drop out, Morwenna. I finished the semester."

"But you're not going back?"

Lord, save me! Maybe God heard; before Bobby

could answer, he heard the crunch of a car's tires on the snow. "Hey, it's Shayne!"

He should feel guilty; his manically depressed brother had arrived. Now, they could all worry about Shayne's problems!

"Yeah, it's Shayne," Morwenna said. She shaded her eyes against the glare on the snow. "He's not alone. Who is that?"

"Think he picked up a hot babe for Christmas?" Bobby asked.

Morwenna elbowed him. "Shayne…with someone he met in the last few days?"

"No, no, too small. It's the kids," Bobby said. "Looks like Connor is in the front, and that's Genevieve in the back."

Shayne stopped the car in the driveway. Bobby thought that the kids were so excited that they had to get out. Connor had just turned nine, and Bobby was sure that the divorce was hard on him. Though Genevieve was just six, it seemed that she actually comprehended the change with the flexibility young children seemed to have.

She jumped out of the car. "Uncle Bobby!" And

rushed him like a guard about to tackle. For a moment he caught his sister's expression. She seemed a little hurt, and a little jealous.

But, then, he'd taken a lot more trouble to make sure that he'd seen his nephew and niece over the years; he knew that Morwenna always meant to.

She was just busy.

"Hey, little one!" Bobby said. He hiked her up on his hip. "Give Aunt Wenna a nice smooch right on the cheek there!"

Genevieve did; and she reached out with a cherubic smile. Morwenna took her, giving her a good hug and a kiss back. She looked at Bobby. Was there even a bit of gratitude in that glance?

Then Connor came flying out of the front, racing to them. He just gave Bobby a hug; Bobby opted not to pick him up. It might be against the boy's dignity. Besides, at nine, Connor was tall and solid.

The car moved on into the garage.

"Didn't know you were coming, munchkins," Bobby said.

"We weren't—then Mommy said we might have

a better time with Daddy. And she said that we might really hurt Gram and Gramps if we didn't come," Connor said.

"Yep, she said that Connor and I were lucky to be loved by so many people," Genevieve said.

Yes, Bobby thought, *his sister-in-law—or ex-sister-in-law—would have said just such a thing, and meant it. She'd never known her own grandparents, and her parents had died the year before she'd met Shayne.*

Shayne had emerged from the car by then and was walking toward them. "Hey, family," he said. He was trying to smile.

"You got the kids!" Morwenna said.

"Yeah. Yeah," Shayne said reflectively. Shayne, Bobby thought, was just as pretty as Morwenna—in a manly sort of way, of course. His brother was a good six foot three with the same dark hair and deep blue eyes. He was fit, and his posture was as straight as an iron girder. He had embraced being a physician, and lived well. Bobby had smoked on and off, over the years; he'd given it up last time because his brother had tortured him so much that the withdrawal was easier than listening to Shayne's speeches.

"That's great," Morwenna said. "That was kind of Cindy."

Shayne sniffed. "Yeah. Kind. She's heading to Europe with the new love of her life. She decided that the kids might be a hindrance."

"Hey!" Morwenna said, frowning. Shayne had the grace to wince, realizing that both his children were there, listening.

Shayne hunkered down by Genevieve. "Hey, guys, remember the rules at Gram's house—you don't come outside without someone here. What's the other rule—do you remember, Connor?"

Connor nodded gravely. "Never take the side path out to the garage or shed in winter. Never. Never, never, never. The snow hides the slope and we could fall and get hurt."

"Good," Shayne said. "Now, Genevieve?"

Genevieve giggled. "Oh, Daddy! We know where the path is!"

"Genevieve, don't come outside without an

adult ever," Shayne said. His voice had taken on an angry tone. "I'm serious."

Connor came closer to his sister. "She knows, Dad. She just likes to argue lately. It's a kid thing."

Shayne nodded, looking at his son with gratitude.

Genevieve hugged him. "I'm sorry, Daddy. I wish Mommy was here, too. She makes good snowmen."

Shayne nodded. "Yes, she makes good snowmen, but she is off on a trip, so we'll have to make do with whatever Uncle Bobby and the rest of us can come up with. Now, run in and give big smooches and hugs to Gram and Gramps, okay? You're going to be the best surprise for them!" Shayne said.

"Shayne," Bobby said quietly. "You've got to be careful."

"I know, I know. Sometimes I can't help it," Shayne said.

"Shayne, damn it. Bobby is right!" Morwenna said firmly. "Cindy is *not* a bad human being, and she was never a bad mother. I told you, she needed more time from you. She held down the fort when the kids were babies—I doubt if you ever changed a diaper—and—"

"Stop it, Morwenna! I changed plenty of diapers," Shayne said. "You weren't around much, so how the hell are you going to tell me what I did and didn't do! I was working—"

"Come on, Wenna," Bobby said. "Shayne was a good dad—you really do work a lot—"

"Better than you, who can't even get the hell through school?" Morwenna interrupted angrily.

Before he could answer, they all froze in silence. They'd heard…*something.*

"What was that?" Morwenna asked. She frowned, turning around. "We're the only shack up here!"

"House," Bobby said.

"Whatever. You have to head down to the lower peak just to get to the tavern," Morwenna said.

"Maybe it was nothing," Shayne said. "Or," he added, giving her a rueful smile, "the voice of God, warning us not to go inside like squabbling children."

"And lay off each other," Bobby added softly. "We are supposed to be adults."

"No...toward the trees," Morwenna said, frowning.

The sound came again. It was definitely a groan.

"There is someone up here," Shayne said. He started walking.

Morwenna ran after him, leaping like a rabbit through the snow. "Shayne, stop. Let me get Dad, and his gun."

"Morwenna, let's see what it is," Bobby said.

"It's a man—I can hear human groans," Shayne said.

Bobby rushed past Morwenna and grabbed her hand. "Come on—he wouldn't be groaning if he was dangerous!"

"It could be a criminal," Morwenna warned.

"Up here? A criminal came all the way up here to groan by our shack? Please!" Bobby said.

Shayne was in the lead, striding through the snow, with Bobby—dragging Morwenna along—following.

Right at the copse that bordered the snow-driven path, there was a man half buried in the drifts. As Shayne hunkered down by him, reaching for a pulse, Bobby studied him.

He appeared to be about thirty, with tawny blood-matted hair and a face with aesthetic contours, although they were half concealed, since he was on his side in the snow.

Good profile, though.

"He's alive," Shayne said. "Steady enough pulse, though it's slow."

"We've got to get him in," Bobby said.

"In! He *could* be a criminal," Morwenna insisted.

"Wenna!" Shayne looked across the fallen body at his sister. "What should I do? Leave him out here to freeze to death? I'm a *doctor*. I can't do that."

"Well, of course, we can't let him freeze to death," Morwenna said. "It's just that…he's a total stranger."

"So what other choice do we have?" Shayne asked.

"Morwenna, it will be okay," Bobby assured her. "Hey, there's a pack of us, and one of him.

It's going to be all right. And Dad does have his shotgun."

"Can he actually shoot?" Morwenna asked.

"Well, I've seen him go skeet shooting," Bobby said, grinning. "I think he hit a few plates."

"What? When?" Morwenna asked.

"When we were kids, remember? We were in Memphis. The parental units brought us all on a canoeing vacation, and we went to see Graceland. It was great, if I recall."

"Yeah," Morwenna said, lowering her eyes. "It was great, wasn't it?" she said softly.

"Doesn't matter right now whether Dad can hit the eye of a needle or miss the side of a barn, it's freezing out here," Shayne said. He had deftly run his hands over the stranger, checking for broken bones or other injuries. "Seems like just his head is bleeding. Maybe he got stranded, got out of his car and fell. God knows, this place has lots of rocks, for certain. Wenna, back up. Bobby, get around over there."

"I'm not puny—I can help," Morwenna said.

"I know that you're the queen of Pilates,

Morwenna, but let Bobby help me right now," Shayne said.

"All right, all right, I'll get the door. Be careful, you two. Maybe he's faking it."

"One, two, three...lift beneath the shoulders," Shayne said.

"Your children are inside that house," Morwenna said worriedly.

"You know he could sue you if we injure him more, Shayne," Bobby said, still not having moved.

"That can't be helped—he'll freeze. He might be in shock...he might well be on the way to hypothermia," Shayne said. "Look, we have to move him, or he'll die."

"I guess that we really have no choice. We can't—"

"No, but...we can't let him just stay here. I guess we can't ask questions or get to know him," Morwenna said.

"I just hope we don't hurt him worse," Bobby said.

Bobby did as his brother instructed, dipping low, and sliding his arm beneath the stranger's back while Shayne carefully did the same from his angle. The stranger groaned again as they managed to get him to his feet.

"It's all right, it's all right!" Shayne said quickly. "We're bringing you in. We're trying to help you."

The man had green eyes, Bobby noted. Strange green eyes. They were actually a greener color than he'd *ever* seen before, and also weirdly translucent.

He noted that Morwenna was staring at the man, looking into his eyes.

And the man was staring back at her.

He managed a single whisper. "Thank you."

She turned and hurried to the house while they followed more slowly with the injured man.

Morwenna opened the door and stood back. Shayne and Bobby staggered toward it, and paused in the doorway, catching their balance.

She looked at Bobby. "Well, this will be different," she said softly. "I can't help but wonder just *who* in the hell we've invited in for Christmas?"

Chapter 2

"What in the name of—" Mike MacDougal began, hurrying into the parlor as his sons stumbled in with the bleeding stranger.

Morwenna looked at her father; she was worried about what they were doing, herself, but to avoid a family argument over Shayne's absolute determination to be a physician at all times, she waved a hand in the air.

"This guy was out there hurt, Dad," she said. "We have to help him."

Stacy, drying her hands on a dish towel, came hurrying into the parlor as well.

"Oh, no! The poor man. Get him onto the sofa, Shayne. Oh, he's bleeding! I'll get a clean wash-cloth and warm water. I'll—" Stacy began.

"Hey!" Mike protested. "Bleeding, in the snow, in the middle of nowhere? How the hell did he get here? How do we know he's not an escaped convict or mass murderer?"

"That's what I said, Dad," Morwenna replied, setting a hand firmly on his chest. "But your son, the physician, refused to allow anyone to bleed to death. Now, Dad—move, please!"

Mike groaned, staring at the man on the sofa. "If you saw everything that I saw, you'd be more careful," he said.

"Dad?" Shayne said.

Genevieve and Connor appeared in the kitchen doorway—just their little heads popping out.

Morwenna hurried toward them. "Hey, little ones. Want to do me a favor? Run upstairs to my bedroom and bring me one of the pillows off my bed. And a blanket, huh? Can you do that?"

They both nodded at her gravely. "Don't worry," Connor told her. "My father will help that man."

"Of course he will," Morwenna said.

She went into the kitchen. Her mother was already filling a basin with warm water; she walked to the pantry and found a stack of fresh linens. "Mom, can I take these?"

Her mother glanced at her. "Of course! You can take anything. The guy's bleeding!"

Stacy was ready with the basin. Morwenna grabbed the towels and they returned to the parlor. Shayne nodded his gratitude and took the basin and the towels. "Looks like he took a good wallop to the side of his head...and there, on his temple. I'm going to need my bag. It's still in the car."

"I'm on it," Bobby said. He turned and exited by the front door.

"Don't just hover!" Shayne said, looking up at Morwenna and his parents as he began to dab carefully at the stranger's wounds. "I think he needs to breathe, too, you know?"

They all stared blankly at him for a minute, and then took a step back.

The kids came clunking down the stairway, bearing a blanket and pillow.

"Good, good, let's get his head propped up," Shayne said. He glanced at his sister, perhaps surprised she'd asked that one of *her* pillows be used for the cause.

She shrugged and watched her older brother as he moved the stranger's head carefully. "His vital signs are growing stronger. I think the blow weakened him and the cold did the rest," he told them. "Of course, I can't make sure he hasn't suffered any serious head trauma until we get him to a hospital."

The stranger stirred. By now, Shayne had washed away the little trails of blood that had streaked down his face.

It was a good face, Morwenna thought. *Nicely chiseled, a bit like the statues she'd seen of Greek and Roman gods. Except, of course, he had a slightly more rugged appeal. Actually, he was a very nice-looking stranger.*

And still a stranger! she warned herself.

They needed him out of their house.

His eyes flew open as she entertained that thought. He was looking straight at her.

She was surprised when she knelt down and touched his cheek. "Hey, it's all right. *You're* all right. We're the MacDougal family. We found you outside in the snow. Do you know who you are? Do you know what you're doing up here? You're hurt."

"Morwenna," Shayne said. "One question at a time for the poor man."

The stranger struggled to sit up and winced. Shayne pressed him back down by the shoulders. "Don't try to get up yet. Let's see how you do. Someone hit you good."

He eased back for a minute, closing his eyes again. "Yeah, someone hit me good. Um…my name is Gabe."

They all looked around at one another. "I'm Gabe," he repeated. "Gabe Lange." He winced, and opened his eyes again. "Could I possibly have some water, please?"

"Water, of course," Stacy said, and turned toward the kitchen.

"Move slowly, and when the water comes, take your first drink slowly," Shayne instructed.

Stacy returned quickly with the water. Morwenna thought that actually, it must have been pretty scary for him to open his eyes, to find all of them looking down at him as if he were an unknown wounded creature they had dragged in.

But, then again, he was.

She glanced at Bobby, who seemed to be a step ahead of her. "Hey, urchins!" he said to Connor and Genevieve. "Let's give your dad the doc some space. I need some help upstairs with presents."

"But...is that guy going to be okay?" Connor asked.

Genevieve's little lips were trembling. Morwenna turned toward her niece. "Yes, of course, my darling. Go on up with Uncle Bobby. The nice man just needs some rest." She glanced at Shayne. Was that all he needed?

"Come on, Lady Niece, Lord Nephew!" Bobby said.

The kids followed him up the stairs.

Morwenna suddenly found herself thinking all

kinds of horrible thoughts. He wasn't all right; he was bleeding internally, and he was going to die on her mother's sofa on Christmas.

She lowered her head quickly. What a horrible concept! A man's life could be in the balance, and she was thinking that his death might affect their Christmas!

The stranger's gaze was on her when she raised her head again. A small smile tugged at his lips as if he had read her thoughts. "I'm strong, really. I'm feeling better already."

"Well, lie still until I've gotten that wound cleaned up," Shayne said firmly.

Gabe winced when Shayne laced the wound with disinfectant, but he didn't let out a sound. "The thing is, you probably do have a concussion," Shayne told him. "You'll need to be careful."

"One of us can stay with him and keep an eye on him," Stacy said.

"I'm going to call an ambulance," Mike told her, speaking up. "Any objections?" he asked. He wasn't speaking to the stranger; he was looking at his wife, daughter and son.

"Not to an ambulance," Shayne assured his father. "What the heck happened to you?"

"Obviously, he got into a fight!" Mike jumped in, his voice harsh.

"I'm with the Virginia State Police," Gabe said. "I was after a man. He eluded me."

"Gabe Lange, with the Virginia State Police?" Mike demanded. Her father sounded as if he was interrogating a prisoner of war. Maybe, in his mind, he was.

"There's nothing to worry about," Gabe assured them. He looked at Morwenna and grimaced. "I was an idiot. I let him get away. But I crawled up here before I passed out. I'm sure that he's long gone. In fact, I'm afraid that he's long gone."

"I'll call that ambulance," Mike said, reaching into his pocket for his cell phone. He stared at Gabe while he dialed. Nothing happened, and he frowned at his phone: "3G, 4G—10G! I don't care how many *Gs* you have, the damned things never work in some places. They're all full of it. Wenna, you're on a different carrier—try your phone."

"Okay, Dad, let me just see where I dropped my

purse," she said. She had dropped it inside, hadn't she? Maybe not.

"I think it's outside," she said.

"Morwenna Alysse MacDougal!" her father said. "What have I taught you about—"

"Hurt guy on the sofa, Dad," Morwenna said. "You always told me that human life was worth more than anything I could possibly own, remember?"

He scowled at her. She hurried outside. She had dropped her purse somewhere out there. It took her a few minutes, but she found it and walked back in the house, pulling her cell phone from it as she did so.

"What number do you want me calling?" she asked.

Mike MacDougal looked at their uninvited guest. "Nine-one-one, of course."

She dialed. She looked at the phone—it, too, said that she was out of range. "Sorry," she told him.

"Well, what the hell is going on?" Mike demanded. "We always have decent satellite coverage up here."

"Dad, calm down—it might be the storm," Shayne told his father.

"Try your phone, Shayne," Mike insisted.

Shayne sighed. He was standing again; he'd patched up Gabe Lange's head nicely, and there was color returning to the man's cheeks. He did look well enough to sit up. He might be entrenched on the couch with her blanket warming him, but she did think then that he must be wet and freezing beneath the covers.

"No bars, Dad. No coverage. It's one hell of a storm brewing up," Shayne said.

Mike snapped his fingers. "Let me see if I can get them out here online!"

He headed for the computer in his office, just down the hall from the stairway.

"Thank you," Gabe told Shayne. "Thank you for patching me up—a stranger on your doorstep."

"Hippocratic oath," Shayne said, grinning. "We're not supposed to trip over the injured and ignore them."

"If I hadn't fallen where I had…if you all hadn't seen me…" Gabe said.

Mike came storming back in from the office. "The goddamn cable is down!" he said irritably.

"Mike! It's Christmas. For the love of *God*—watch your language!" Stacy said.

"Mom, Dad, *please,* both of you!" Morwenna murmured.

"Dad, you don't need the cops anyway—he *is* a cop," Shayne said.

"Likely story!" Mike said.

"Mike!" Stacy gasped.

"Dad!" Shayne and Morwenna said in unison.

They didn't deter their father at all. He turned on Gabe Lange. "I have a shotgun in this house, and I know how to use it. I'm a district attorney in Philadelphia, young man, and I know my way around crooks. And if you're a cop, where's your gun? Eh? Where's your uniform?"

"My gun was lost quickly—I try never to use firearms. Innocent people get hurt as often as the bad guys, so it seems. But, yeah, I carry a weapon. Now it's gone, somewhere in a bush halfway up the mountainside," Gabe said. "Look, sir, I'm not here to hurt anyone, I swear it!"

"And so the devil swears!" Mike muttered, and walked away.

"Sorry, the lawyer side of my husband is always angry. But he's a really good man," Stacy told Gabe Lange. Then, she suddenly thrust her hand forward. "I'm Stacy, my husband is Mike. Your real live doctor is Shayne, and this is our daughter, Morwenna. She's an artist and advertising exec. She took business as well as art. Don't you think that was incredibly smart? She is able to use her talent *and* keep a job, and—"

"Mom!" Morwenna said, interrupting her quickly. She glared at her mother, meaning, *Let's not just air the family laundry.*

"He doesn't need a dossier on all of us!" she added and laughed to soften the statement. "To finish the introductions in the family, my little brother is Bobby, and Shayne's kids are named Connor and Genevieve. Welcome to our home for Christmas. I'm so sorry about what happened to you. Won't your family be worried?"

Gabe looked away from her for a moment. "I have a huge extended family, but my immediate family wasn't expecting me. They'll be fine without me—there's a lot of work that goes on tonight. I'm grateful that you've taken me in."

Shayne squeezed his shoulder. "I would be happier if you were in a hospital," he said.

Gabe pushed back the blanket and sat up, despite Shayne's protests. "I'm not even dizzy anymore. I swear," he said. "I'm not sure I'd want to hit the ring for a few bouts or anything, but I'm doing fine."

"Then sit."

"I'm sitting," Gabe said.

His teeth began to chatter.

Shayne brought out his little light, and told Gabe to follow the beam. He inspected their guest's eyes with a serious expression, then let out a sigh and shrugged. "Your pupils are showing no signs of a possible problem."

"He's fine, but he's freezing," Morwenna said. "He must be soaked."

"Oh, how very rude of us," Stacy said. She

looked at her oldest son. "Shayne, there must still be jeans and T's and flannel shirts up in your room. Can you loan something to Mr. Lange?"

"Gabe, please," their visitor insisted. "I *am* on your sofa."

"Of course." Shayne seemed troubled, but he shook his head. "We'll head up to my old room. You can get out of those wet clothes, take a shower and then put on something dry and warm."

"That would be great. My most sincere gratitude to you all," Gabe said.

"I'll give you a hand getting up," Shayne said. "Use the banister—I'll support you on the other side."

Morwenna hovered, watching as they started up the stairs. "Great kids," Gabe told Shayne.

He didn't ask about their mother; somehow, Shayne volunteered information.

"Yes, they're great kids. They've stayed that way through the divorce," Shayne said.

"Most important thing to remember in a divorce—your children still have you both as parents, the people they love most in the world. I'm glad to hear that you and your ex are respecting one another. You should be proud."

Morwenna didn't get to hear her brother's answer; they were already up the stairs.

Her father emerged from the kitchen, a glass in his hand.

"What the hell is going on?" he demanded.

"Honestly, Mike, it's Christmas!" Stacy said.

"Shayne is giving him something to wear that isn't soaked with snow," Morwenna said.

"I'm getting the shotgun," Mike said. "I just don't trust that guy. I'm going to have it on hand at all times."

Genevieve, unsurprisingly for her age, was not an ace at wrapping packages. In a few instances when he didn't cut the paper quickly enough, she cut pieces that were too small. Small items, stocking stuffers, were wrapped in enough paper to conceal a small elephant.

"Wow, there's a lot of stuff here!" Connor told Bobby, his eyes wide. Then they clouded. "I guess we won't get much here," he added.

"We won't get presents?" Genevieve asked.

"Of course you'll get presents," Bobby told him.

But Connor shook his head knowingly. "We did get presents, Genevieve. Remember? Daddy and Gram and all sent them before, and we opened them at home." He looked at his uncle apologetically. "We got good presents, Uncle Bobby. Gram likes to give presents, huh—is that why there are so many here?"

"Gram has always loved to make everyone a stocking," Bobby said, "including Gramps. But I wouldn't worry—you'll get presents."

"Yes!" Genevieve said. She had a little lisp. Her front tooth was loose. "Santa Claus will come here, right?"

Shayne knew that Connor didn't believe in Santa Claus, so he brought a finger to his lips and winked.

"That's right. And Santa Claus can find any house," he assured Genevieve.

Connor rolled his eyes. "Yeah, sure."

Shayne poked his head in the doorway. "Hey,

Bobby, thanks. Want to take over in my room for a minute?"

"Sure. Take over what?"

"Watching our—guest. The guy we picked up—Gabe—is freezing. The snow soaked through his clothing. I've got him in my room, but I need you to stand by the door while I dig in my closet for something for him to wear."

"I can find him something—" Bobby said.

"No, that's cool, I still have you by an inch or so in the shoulder and chest region, and the guy looks like he's about my size. I just don't want to leave him standing there. Connor, you can watch your sister for a minute, huh?"

"Yeah, sure, Dad," Connor said. He made a face. "Bobby still has scissors from when he was in grade school. Can you believe that Gram keeps stuff that long?" he asked with a laugh. "I'll watch her, but I don't think Genevieve can hurt herself."

"I can cut paper!" Genevieve announced proudly.

Shayne walked over to ruffle his son's hair. "Thanks," he said. "And, of course you know how to cut paper, Genevieve. You're a very bright little girl."

"Mommy taught me," she said.

"Yell if you need me," Bobby said, rising quickly to follow his brother out to the hall and to Shayne's room. *Shayne's room. None of them lived there anymore; actually, they'd never lived there. Well, Mom had, and they had often spent summer months and spring and Christmas breaks there. This place evoked a lot of good memories. His parents were in Philadelphia, Shayne was in Pittsburgh and Morwenna was in New York. Not that far, as the world went. But this was where they had always gathered.*

Where it seemed their mother had created a memorial to the past, when they'd actually been a family.

Bobby was suddenly ashamed of his thoughts. They *were* a family.

The bathroom door was ajar.

"He took a serious crack on the head," Shayne said when Bobby crooked a brow at him. "He could fall—he could need help. Look, none of us are in high school football anymore. Just hang around outside the door and be ready to rush in if you hear him slip or scream or rip out the shower curtain, huh?"

"Fine, I'll be ready," Bobby said. He leaned against the wall by the door that was an inch or so open. The water started to spray.

He heard his brother fumbling around in the closet. Shayne emerged. "I'm just going down to toss this stuff in the dryer—freshen it up. I'll be right back."

"Big bro, you're the M.D. Don't be gone long," Bobby said.

"Two minutes. Just going to toss the stuff around because it's been in a closet," Shayne said. Two minutes? Hell! What if something happened? What if the guy did fall? Shayne was right—they weren't accustomed to showering in a mass steam room of sweat anymore.

Awkward.

He could hear the shower spray, and nothing else.

He tapped lightly on the door. "You all right in there?" he asked.

"Yep, fine, thanks."

"Yell, if—"

"Thanks!"

Bobby was startled when the shower stopped. He backed into the foot of his brother's bed and sat with a plop.

Gabe Lange came out from the bathroom, one towel tied around his waist as he used a second to dry his hair.

"I can't tell you how good it feels to be warm," Gabe said.

"Ah, great. Yeah. I can imagine."

"Are you from here? Winter can be pretty brutal, huh?"

"My mom is actually from here. I was born in Philadelphia. We were all born in Philadelphia. I mean, Shayne, Morwenna and I," Bobby said. "What about you?"

"Down in the city," Gabe said. "Richmond."

"Nice. So—how did you come to be out here in the mountains?" Bobby asked.

"State police—we go wherever. Within the state, of course. So, are you a college student?" Gabe asked him.

Bobby couldn't help but roll his eyes. "Yes, and no. I've just applied again. I've been to Columbia and Northwestern."

"Those are good schools. Where are you trying to go now?"

The question was entirely innocent, and a natural get-to-know-you question. Bobby looked at the door; he didn't want Shayne to hear him.

"They don't know it—none of them know it—I applied to Juilliard."

"Ah. For—"

"I'm a guitarist, and I want to write my own music," Bobby said, warmth entering his voice; he was speaking quickly. "My family—they're all superachievers. My dad could write his ticket anywhere, though he's stayed with the D.A.'s office. Maybe he'll run for something someday, who knows? My brother is, as you know, an M.D., and my sister, bless her heart, is an executive with one of Manhattan's finest ad agencies. All respectable moneymakers."

"And are they happy?" Gabe asked him.

"Well, yeah, I think. Shayne loves medicine.

I know—through the years—that my folks have talked about his work every time he got an offer to go into private practice. And Morwenna..."

"Yeah?"

"She was an artist once. A really good artist."

"Doesn't she get to use that talent at the ad agency?"

"I think that was the idea. But I think it got lost in one of the executive meetings," Bobby said wryly. "I loved it when I was a kid. She was always drawing fantasy creatures for me. Being snowed in up here isn't really anything all that new. It's happened before. God forbid they sell this place and head south!"

"Would you want them to?" Gabe asked him.

Bobby thought about that for a minute. "Palm Springs, Daytona Beach...snowbound mountains!" He laughed. "No, I don't suppose I would want them to sell. The house is historic—really historic. You can tell by the horrible plumbing and the really bad electricity. But the place really means something to my mom. And, in all honesty, I guess it means something to me, too."

"That's nice to hear. But, what's the story with your music?" Gabe asked.

"According to my father, music is a hobby. Not a career. You go to school for a career." Bobby looked at the door again. "I'm an adult. If I really want it, I can just stop taking parental financial aid and go it on my own. It will be much harder, but I'm willing to give it go. The thing is…" Bobby trailed off.

"Yeah?" Gabe pressed.

He laughed suddenly. "I guess it's a good thing. We fight like cats and dogs, and it's hard to plan a family dinner with a pack of overachievers…but, still, my parents always loved us. It's the way that they look at me that kills me. It's the disappointment." Bobby shut up, wondering why the hell he had just kind of spilled out so much to a stranger. Maybe, he thought, because he'd needed to tell someone, but he didn't want to tell them until he knew what might happen. He knew the odds were against him; getting into Juilliard was a numbers game, and there could only be so many people who got into the school. There were other music schools—if he didn't make it, he'd try again.

But he didn't want to tell anyone in the house that he'd auditioned. He didn't want them to see his hope, or, his disappointment if he didn't make it. Even though it meant they were sure to lecture him through the holiday, he was sticking with the story that he'd gotten a job working in New York City for the coming semester, until he figured out just what he did want. It wasn't a lie; he did have a job offer working with a group of musical waiters at a place called Napoli. They waited on tables, stopped, picked up their instruments and did quick numbers in between.

Even if he made it into Juilliard, Mario, the head of the group and a great vocalist, had assured him they'd be happy to work with his schedule.

It was all okay, really. But he could just hear his father's voice: "A singing waiter? What kind of life is that, Bobby? What if you want a family, kids? There's no advancement, Bobby. Nowhere to go."

"Sounds to me like you know how to get where you want to go—just have to hang in and take those first steps. So," he said loudly, "Christmas here every year, huh?"

Bobby realized that Shayne was coming back with clothing for their guest.

He'd told a stranger, and not his brother, what he was hoping to do with his life.

"Yep, every year," he said.

As Shayne walked in, Bobby walked out. "Patient seems to be fine," he said.

Back in his own room, he found Genevieve and Connor sitting in the midst of a massive pile of wrapping-paper scraps. Rudolph was dancing here and there, and little blue snowflakes lay in strips across the floor.

"Nice job," he said cheerfully. He looked around at the mess. "I think I hear Gram calling you from the kitchen!"

He led them back past his brother's door, and could hear the drone of Shayne's voice. No surprise. Shayne was willing to talk about the difficulty of the divorce at the drop of a hat.

Except that Shayne didn't seem to be doing all

the talking. He stopped speaking now and then, and Bobby could hear the stranger's voice.

That he was speaking wasn't odd at all.

That Shayne apparently stopped speaking to actually listen was odd indeed.

Chapter 3

"Dinner's ready!" Morwenna called up the stairs.

Her father had been in his study and he emerged, slipping an arm around her shoulders. "So, kid, what happened? I thought we were going to get to meet Mr. Perfect this year."

"He couldn't come, Dad, and he isn't Mr. Perfect."

"But he's a major presence in your life, right?" her father asked her.

"Dad, we've been seeing each other about six

months. He still has his apartment, I still have mine. I—"

"I should hope so!" Mike said, disgruntled.

Morwenna chuckled softly. "Dad! You'd be surprised at the mismatched couples that jump in together in New York. The cost of living is staggering. But we're both doing well, and he's really a nice guy."

"So nice that he isn't here with you at Christmas," her father said. He shook his head, crossing his arms over his chest. She had seen him in the courtroom, standing in just that position, when he was arguing the guilt of an accused.

He was good at the stance.

"Dad, an entire group from our agency was going to Cancún. Alex put the trip together before he knew that I was coming home."

"And a bunch of adults couldn't go to Cancún without him?"

"Hey! I'm an adult, too. I could have gone with them."

Mike MacDougal shook his head sadly and sagely.

"No, because you know that you would break your mother's heart if you did something like that."

"When people are together—married, cohabiting, etcetera—they often go to one family one year, and another family the next. And children of divorced parents sometimes wind up so confused they don't know where to go anymore—so they head to Cancún."

Mike was silent, shaking his head for a minute, and then said, "Here's the only truth I know—we're all going to die. You can even get out of the 'taxes' part of death and taxes. And when we die, there's only one thing we take with us."

"What's that?"

"Love," Mike said, tapping his heart. "You and your siblings will talk about your mother and me when we're gone, and that way, we'll still be alive. Love lives on—not trips to Cancún, fruity drinks imbibed on a beach, or expensive clothing, or even a hotshot job. Your family loves you…you deserve a guy who knows about family, and love."

Morwenna stared at her father, stunned. She'd never heard such a speech from him before.

"You were the one who pushed me through school," she reminded him. "Then it was, 'We all have to be independent, make our mark in life! There's no one you can depend on but yourself.' I went to school. I learned how to negotiate, engage a client, play all the business games. I even own stock, for God's sake."

She was surprised when he didn't laugh, or at least crack a smile.

"Christmas," he said softly, "always makes me kind of sentimental."

He walked past her. Bobby came down the stairs, followed by Shayne, the kids and their strange guest, Gabe Lange.

"What's up? What's with that look?" Bobby asked her.

"Dad. Our father has gotten all weird," she whispered, looking past him with a careful smile. "Christmas Eve dinner is on, Mr. Lange."

He looked even better. Despite looking a bit worse for wear, the guy really did have a great face, all the right bone structure in place, but a face that wasn't too pretty, and the structure didn't take away from the strength of his jawline. In Shayne's flannel shirt and old jeans, he looked like a sandy-haired woodsman. He could have done a commercial for some kind of rugged men's cologne.

She reminded herself that many a serial killer had offered the world a pleasant face. She still didn't trust him. He was a stranger in their midst.

"Thank you," he told her. "Thank you for having me in your home like this. Christmas is a special time. I didn't really mean to intrude," he told her.

"Well, I guess you didn't collapse by our house on purpose," Morwenna said dryly. "Come along."

She led the way from the parlor along the hall to the dining room, attached to the kitchen. Her mom was directing their extra guests to take their seats.

They hadn't expected Shayne's kids, and they certainly hadn't expected Gabe Lange, but her mother could always manage to make a meal stretch. Turkey would be the main course tomorrow. For Christmas Eve, Stacy always cooked a strange conglomeration of food—linguini with clam sauce, and potatoes and rice, a roast, broccoli with hollandaise sauce, green beans with slivered almonds, a massive "kitchen sink" salad and bread pudding. Perhaps the meal stretched so well because there were so many items to be had.

Morwenna looked at her mother. "What else? What can I get? What can I do?"

"Drinks," her mother said, setting the bowl with the linguini on the table. "Take a tally. Kids, are you having juice? What would you like?"

They were all startled when Genevieve answered with a little sniff. "I would like Mommy to be here," she said.

The adults froze. Connor placed his arm around his sister. "She's on a trip. We'll see her again soon," he said.

Morwenna dived in quickly, not wanting Shayne to say anything. She knew he couldn't understand what had happened to his marriage, and that he didn't intend to hurt the kids. He also couldn't help but be bitter.

"I'll bet she'll come back with great and wonderful gifts!" Morwenna said, walking around to hug Genevieve. "So, until then, what will you have to drink?"

"Can we have soda, Dad?" Connor asked.

"It's Christmas Eve, why not?" Shayne told his son. Morwenna caught her brother's eyes. He smiled at her; he was not going to make a disparaging remark about his ex-wife. Something about him seemed to have changed, just since he'd gotten to the house. Maybe he'd had a long talk with Bobby upstairs.

"Two sodas… Bobby? Soda, beer, wine?"

"Hey, it's my first 'legal' Christmas. Please serve me a lovely glass of Cabernet," Bobby said. "And Dad can't even get arrested, or call the cops himself, because I am legal these days!"

"I'd have myself arrested?" Mike asked.

"Yeah, I think you would, Dad. In the name of justice for all!" He laughed. "My dad may be the best assistant D.A. in the country. I think he would have himself arrested under the innkeeper law," he told Gabe.

Mike groaned. "You were underage—you and your friends. It's illegal for an adult to aid a young person in securing alcoholic beverages. Now you are twenty-one. Go for it."

"Tough to grow up in such a household," Shayne told Gabe.

"Not so bad. We just decided to smoke pot, since everything was illegal for us," Bobby said cheerfully.

Mike looked as if he would explode.

"Chill, Dad, chill, just kidding!" Bobby said.

"An honest man. Rare to find," Gabe said. He had a curious expression. "I think I'd like a beer, if I may. Sounds intriguing—um, good, sorry. Sounds good."

The seeds of mistrust settled more deeply into Morwenna's soul. *Intriguing? Beer? Where the hell had this guy been? Locked up somewhere?*

"Mom, Dad, Shayne?" Morwenna asked.

In the end, she had two caffeine-free sodas, four glasses of wine and two bottles of beer. She moved into the kitchen to get the drinks, and found herself pausing to look around.

And feel guilty.

Stacy even cleaned while she cooked. With all that she had prepared, her mother had kept up with pots and other utensils as well. She had done so much; every year she did so much. She'd always been an at-home mom. Morwenna wondered if she had ever had her own set of dreams, and if their father's career had changed Stacy's life. She'd always cooked breakfast, made lunches, driven the children to Girl Scouts, Boy Scouts and Little League, sewn costumes, bought the candy, gone trick-or-treating and done everything imaginable.

Stacy followed her into the kitchen. "I'll get the sodas," she said. "If you pour the wine."

"Mom, why don't you just sit, and let me do this."

"Are you kidding? I'm in my element, sweetheart. And we don't get days like these often anymore—you know, when I have all of you!"

Morwenna walked to the counter where her mother was pouring the sodas. She slipped her arms around her waist. "Mom, did you ever want to really do anything? I mean, you know, have a career—do something else besides wait on Dad and all of us?"

Stacy turned to stare at her, her eyes wide. "Morwenna, *this* is my career, my life."

"But, did Dad stop you from having any other dreams? Now would be the time to fulfill a dream. It's never too late, you know."

She was surprised; she was trying to stand up for her mother, and her mother was angry. "You get it out of your head that your father stopped me from doing anything. Because of your father, I could live my dream, I could have *this* career."

"But we're gone now, Mom. We're all gone, out of the house, grown up."

"And that means you're not my children anymore?"

"But Dad pushed me so hard to make sure that I had a career—" Morwenna began.

Stacy quickly cut her off. "Your father pushed *you,* yes, because you needed more. And because the world is changing. Now two people have to work sometimes in order to afford to raise a family. I guess you don't understand. You have all your sleek, chic clothing, designer briefcases and all-important meetings. And I concentrate on making sure a roast is edible. But, Morwenna, don't try to fix me. I like what I am, and I like what I do, and there are ups and downs in life all the time, but I'm *happy*. Maybe your ex-sister-in-law is the only one who really knows that, since she made sure that the kids came here for Christmas. The only one who appreciates family, it seems, is the one no longer in the family!"

Morwenna didn't have a chance to respond; Stacy expertly balanced the four wineglasses and seemed to sail out of the kitchen, her head held regally high.

"I wanted to draw!" she said, aware that her mother couldn't hear her. "I wanted to draw, and paint, and create things!"

She hesitated, aware that, supposedly, the job she had taken would allow her to do just that. But she had become a stereotype of corporate America instead.

"I like my clothes!" she told the swinging door. She tucked two bottles of beer under her arm, picked up the sodas and followed Stacy back to the dinner table.

"Ah, Morwenna is here now. We can say grace," Stacy said.

Mike stood and looked around the table. "Thank you, Lord, for the food we are about to eat. Thank you for the safety and lives of our family. Amen."

"Nice," Gabe commented.

"Better than the old joke, eh, of just saying '*Grace*'!" Bobby teased.

"We know better than to give the task to you, son," Mike said, but he was grinning.

"Wait!" Genevieve said. "Wait, Gram, please! Can we do that thing that Mommy's family does?"

They all looked at her. Genevieve grinned and stood up. She took Bobby's hand and reached for her brother's.

"Ah, Genevieve, what are you doing?" Connor demanded.

"Give me your hand, Connor. I don't have any cooties!" Genevieve said.

Connor shrugged and gave her his hand. "This is just silly. Mom isn't here."

"Hey, your sister wants to have your mom here—in spirit," Shayne said. "And let's all try to make each other happy, huh?"

Genevieve grinned happily. "Okay, everybody, now, *shake a lot of love!*"

Around the table, they held hands, and on Genevieve's command, they all shook their hands up and down.

"Now," Genevieve said complacently, "it's almost kind of Christmas!"

"They don't even really know what day Christmas Day is supposed to be," Connor said. "Some popes or priests somewhere got together to pick a day."

"That's right, Connor," Gabe said. "But it doesn't take away from the fact that the day was chosen, and it's the day when Christians celebrate the birth of Jesus. So, it's the chosen day, and your sister is right—it's almost here."

"So it might have been any day," Morwenna murmured. Except that she was heard. She looked at Gabe, who was staring at her with amusement.

"What? It's a day for miracles or the like?" she asked him softly.

"Miracles are what we make ourselves," he said. He looked upward. "Maybe the Lord can lend a hand, but we have to create magic ourselves."

She groaned softly. "A do-gooder cop. Great."

He just grinned. She did, too.

And, somehow, the meal went along with the conversation pleasant instead of strained, with the family asking questions instead of throwing out accusations, and her father actually asked Bobby to bring out his guitar when they got to the bread pudding.

He played Christmas carols and the family chimed in, except for Morwenna.

Gabe looked at her. "Are you really that 'bah, humbug'?" he asked her.

"No. I sound like a wounded hyena when I sing," she told him.

"But these are Christmas carols. Everyone sings Christmas carols." He looked upward again. "He doesn't care what you sound like."

Morwenna laughed. "I think I'll pick up the plates."

She was surprised when he caught her hand. "'O Little Town of Bethlehem,'" he said. "I know you know it. I'll help with the plates. One song, huh?"

With an exaggerated sigh, she sat again. She sang along with the family, watching Gabe. "See?"

"I thought you were great."

She drew back, looking at him suspiciously. "Do you actually have a family?" she asked him.

"I do. I have a wonderful family," he assured her.

"Why aren't you going crazy, trying to find a working phone?" she demanded. "You're not with them."

"Because I'm not the kind to beat my head against the wall when something can't work," he told her.

She wanted to argue the point, but she really couldn't. The storm had done nothing but grow stronger in the hours since she had arrived, and it did seem that they had lost all phone connections. Were the satellites all snowbound as well?

"No television for the kiddies," she murmured. "No computer games."

"Bobby, play 'Silent Night' for me, please?" Stacy asked.

Bobby looked over at his mother. "Sure, Mom. I thought you didn't care for the song on a guitar that much. You always like it on piano."

"And one of these days, I'm going to get one here," she assured him. "But, please, play it for me."

"Nothing like a rock version of 'Silent Night,'" Mike said.

Of course, Bobby heard him.

"I'd love to hear it, too," Morwenna said. "Scrooge can go into the kitchen!"

They all managed to laugh at that, even Mike. And Bobby played. Gabe sang the song alone this time with a clear, smooth, fluid tenor voice that was absolutely beautiful. When the song was over, everyone at the table just stared at him.

"Wow," Bobby said.

"That was all you. You can really play," Gabe said.

Fearful that a fight would begin over Bobby's

music versus his college education, Morwenna quickly rose. "Let's get the plates into the kitchen," she said.

"Really, kids, I'm fine," Stacy said.

Morwenna looked at her mother. "Mom, please let us help. Remember, you don't get all of us that often and we want to be with you—if we help, we're with you."

Stacy nodded, but looked at Connor and Genevieve. "Shayne, maybe you could read the kids a story. I'm afraid that we have no internet and we're not getting television reception, either."

"No cable?" Connor asked, horrified.

"Yes, but that's okay. We can do other things to have fun!" Stacy said.

Shayne looked blankly back at his mother. Morwenna felt her heart contract. Shayne was too much like her; they both worked so much they didn't really know how to have fun.

Just as that thought struck her, Bobby piped up. "I know what we'll do! Auntie Morwenna will draw up a Christmas creature, and we'll make up a story about it as we go along."

"Doesn't anyone have an iPad?" Connor asked hopefully.

Yes, actually, she did, Morwenna thought.

But Bobby was looking at her hopefully. She smiled. She really loved her little brother. He might be the ne'er-do-well of the group, but he had heart. She winced inwardly. *And he did have talent. But Dad was overprotective and mistrustful of everyone. He'd worked with too many crooks. In his mind, too, he'd let too many go free. So had they fallen back on their father's words too many times because they were afraid of taking chances? Afraid of having faith in their own abilities?*

"Plates in the kitchen!" Morwenna said. "We all help Mom, and then we'll do a whole Christmas story of our own in the parlor!"

As she passed Shayne with plates, he caught her arm. "You really don't have your iPad?" he asked hopefully.

"Shayne MacDougal, believe it or not, the artist in me loves a pencil and paper, and we're going to play," she said. "Difficult, I know. But your kids will love it, and you don't have to be embarrassed. Hey, you can play a monster."

She hurried by her brother. *Shayne loved his job. He just needed to realize that his loved ones needed healing as much as his patients.*

With everyone helping, it was quick work getting the table cleared. Luckily, the dishwasher and electricity were still functioning, so within twenty minutes, food was stowed, plates and glasses and serving pieces rinsed and set to wash and the kitchen squeaky clean.

Mike asked his sons for help with the logs; they rebuilt the fire in the parlor. They managed to do so, only jokingly taunting one another as they shared the labor.

But, before they could start, Stacy turned back to the kitchen. "We have to have hot cocoa for the performance."

Bobby groaned. "You'd think we were starving, Ma."

"She likes to have the fire—and her kids drinking cocoa," Morwenna said.

"Spike mine, Ma," Bobby called.

When cocoa was finished—spiked for the adults, plain old cocoa for the kids—Bobby ushered his mother back to the sofa. He hiked Genevieve over his head, and then set her on his mother's lap.

Morwenna hurried to her room and found one of her old sketchbooks and quickly looked up something she had created years before— Magala, the Christmas elf. She ran back downstairs with the sketchbook. "Bobby, you get to be Wager, the traveling troubadour." She frowned, and then looked at Gabe, who was waiting expectantly. "Gabe, you can play Magala, the Christmas elf," she said, and showed him the picture. "And, Shayne, you get to be Mr. Mean, the Abominable Snowman who lives by the workshop at the North Pole."

"Great!" Shayne said.

But Connor giggled, and Shayne flashed his son a smile. He lifted his arms in a huge Abominable Snowman pose.

"Who are you, Aunt Morwenna?" Genevieve asked, cuddling her teddy bear as she sat on her grandmother's lap.

"The narrator," Morwenna said. "Hang on just one minute." Glancing at her pictures, she scurried first to the kitchen. She found a new mop head and came back to put it on Shayne's head, which delighted the kids further. But Shayne wasn't complete until she had whitened his face with cold cream. The more Shayne groaned, the more his kids laughed, and she was happy when she saw him smile—despite the goop on his face.

Bobby had secured one of his old Robin Hood hats from a long-gone Renaissance festival, and for Gabe, Morwenna found an old pair of Halloween ears. They were ready.

"Intro!" Morwenna told Bobby. He strummed a light tune that grew dark.

"Once upon a time, up at the North Pole, there lived a good elf named Magala," Morwenna said.

Gabe got into the action, leaping up, smiling and bowing. It was good; he didn't seem to have suffered any real damage from his fight in the snow.

"He worked all day at creating toys for children," Morwenna continued.

Gabe pantomimed the creation of a bicycle, and

everyone laughed as he kept turning the invisible instruction sheet around and around.

"But, nearby, in the darkest, dankest cave, lived Mr. Mean, the Abominable Snowman," Morwenna said.

Bobby played a few dark and threatening chords as Shayne stood up, lifted his arms and shoulders in a huge display of strength.

"I'm mean!" Shayne said. He looked at Morwenna. "How am I mean? What do I do?"

"While Magala works day and night, trying to make a wonderful Christmas for children everywhere, Mr. Mean plans to destroy all the toys!" Morwenna said.

Bobby played even darker music.

Shayne walked over to Gabe, stared at him and picked up the imaginary bike. He threw it to the ground and then hopped up and down on it.

"That's what I always felt like doing with those instruction sheets," Mike said softly, drawing laughter from all of them.

"Daddy, you're so mean!" Genevieve said, delighted.

"And I just stare at him while he ruins Christmas?" Gabe asked.

"No! Here's the thing—Mr. Mean goes away all proud of himself for having taken care of Christmas. But, you see, Magala is a magic elf, and as soon as Mr. Mean is gone, he just puts the bicycle back together again, and he does it double time," Morwenna said.

The children were delighted as Gabe tried to perform all his actions again in double time.

"So, all the toys were ready to go, to be placed in Santa's sleigh," Morwenna said.

Gabe put his hands on his hips and nodded proudly.

"But!" Morwenna said, and Bobby strummed out a dire musical warning.

"Mr. Mean came in and stomped on the toys again!"

Big-armed and growling, Shayne grabbed the imaginary bike, tossed it to the floor and hopped up and down, his dramatic antics growing with each jump.

"And then what happened?" Connor demanded, clearly drawn in.

"Magala didn't have any presents for Santa's sleigh!" Genevieve said.

"Ah, but you see, he did," Gabe told her.

"But the bike is smashed to bits," Connor protested.

"Smashed, yeah, broken. But all the pieces were there," Gabe said, flashing Morwenna a quick smile.

"So," Morwenna said, "Magala the elf picked up all the pieces, and when the children awoke in the morning, they realized that they hadn't just gotten a present—they'd gotten a puzzle, too. They just had to work together and connect the pieces."

Genevieve, with wide and innocent eyes, leaped up and ran over to stand by the imaginary bike.

"My dad could put it back together. Especially when he's not being Mr. Mean!" Genevieve said.

"Ah, yes. And there's the magic to the Christmas story," Morwenna said. "When Mr. Mean realized that he couldn't break something that can't be seen or touched—like the love shared at Christmas—he gave up being Mr. Mean, and he became Mr. Nice, and he went about the country, finding children who didn't have fathers, and helping them put all their toys back together again!"

Bobby strummed the guitar. "The end!" he announced.

"The end, and time for little people to go to bed," Shayne said. "Morwenna—"

"Absolutely, my beautiful little niece is in with me," Morwenna said.

"And I'll take Connor, and—"

"Gabe can have the lower bunk in my room," Bobby said.

"But for now...young'uns, to bed! Santa can't come if you don't go to bed," Shayne said firmly.

"I'm not that young," Connor protested, standing tall to prove his point.

"Hey—Uncle Bobby worked hard on that tree. And your grandmother baked cookies for Santa. You're going to go to bed, and Santa is going to come," Morwenna said. She was surprised when Connor looked at her, blushed, lowered his head and smiled.

"Alrighty, Auntie Wenna," Connor said. "I like playing your games. I'll think of it that way."

"That's wonderfully mature, Connor," she told him.

"Kiss Gramps and Gram, and let's go on up," Morwenna suggested.

Connor kissed his family, and Genevieve followed him around. When he reached Gabe, Connor somberly shook his hand.

"And a good night to you, young man," Gabe said.

Genevieve impulsively gave Gabe a kiss on the cheek. He smiled. "Thank you. And good night, Genevieve. I have a feeling you'll go through life fixing the things that need to be fixed, young lady. You have a good night's sleep."

"It works when we all fix stuff, huh?" Genevieve asked.

Gabe grinned. "Just like magic," he agreed.

"Come on, come on up," Morwenna urged the two. Shayne probably had the kids' presents out in the car, in the garage, and the storm was still pounding them. It was going to be a trick to get everything in. She was worried, too, about what they'd find in the house to give the children so that they had something to wake up to; they'd sent the family presents on ahead to Cindy a few weeks ago, since she was going to have the children for Christmas at that time, and Shayne for the New Year's weekend.

"I'm good, Auntie Wenna," Connor said at the door to Bobby's room. "I'm cool. I can put myself to bed."

She hesitated. He reminded her of a brave little warrior standing there.

"Both your parents love you very much, Connor," she told him.

He nodded. "Yeah, well, I just need to learn to handle things on my own. I've got Genevieve to think about."

Morwenna smiled and ruffled his hair. "Good night, Connor. Love you."

"Love you, too, Auntie Wenna," he said.

She brought Genevieve into her room, stood with her while she washed her face and brushed her teeth, helped her into an old flannel gown of her own that was far too big, but which Genevieve wanted to wear, and sat at the foot of the bed.

"Say prayers with me, Auntie Wenna?" she asked.

"Um, sure," Morwenna said a little awkwardly. She smiled; as a child, she had gotten down on her knees at night and told God all her problems. As an adult, she'd figured out that he was busy with more serious issues, such as war, starvation and disease.

When had she gotten to a point where she believed that she had to fight alone against the world? When she'd figured out hers was just a little life, a grain in the sands of time.

She knelt down next to her niece and folded her hands prayer fashion.

"Dear God. Happy birthday to baby Jesus— whatever his birthday might be. We love him, no matter when it is. Please keep my mommy and daddy safe, and Auntie Wenna, Uncle Bobby, Gram and Gramps. And don't worry about toys for me this Christmas. Honest." She opened her eyes for a moment to take a sideways glance at

Morwenna. "Auntie Morwenna will let me play with some of her stuff, so I'm really good. Oh, thank you for the bread pudding. It was especially yummy. Amen."

"Nice prayer, young lady. Good night."

"Aren't you going to say your prayers?" Genevieve asked her.

She looked at her niece for a moment. In her head, thoughts she couldn't say out loud in front of the child—or anyone—swirled into a prayer. *Dear God, please don't make it that I am an idiot; that Alex really wants to be with me 'cause he believes I'm on the top rungs of the professional ladder, and that he isn't in Cancún, chasing after Double-D Debbie from Accounting on the beach....*

She gave herself a mental shake and folded her hands again. "Dear God, thank you for my brothers, my mom and dad, and especially my nephew, Connor, and my niece, Genevieve. Guard them for me, please, through whatever life offers." She hesitated a minute. "Help me be a better, more understanding me."

Genevieve nudged her. "And happy birthday to baby Jesus."

"Yes, of course. Happy birthday to baby Jesus."

"And may we all get back together again. My mom and dad," Genevieve said, looking upward again.

Morwenna rose and lifted Genevieve, hugging her. "Sometimes, honey, that just can't happen. What you need to know is how much they both love you and Connor."

"How can they love anybody when they hate each other so much?" Genevieve asked her.

"They don't hate each other."

"They sure act like it sometimes," Genevieve said.

"They—they're just angry because they… they…"

"They didn't know how to fix things," Genevieve said. "That's why I really prayed that we could learn to fix things."

"Praying for miracles," Morwenna murmured.

Genevieve smiled sadly at her. "Well, fixing things is like a miracle."

"Yes, it is, sweetie, yes, it is," Morwenna agreed. She tucked Genevieve into her bed, pulling the covers close. "I'll leave the bathroom light on, okay, kid? And the door ajar."

"Good night," Genevieve said. "Don't let the bedbugs bite."

"Let's hope not. We'll have the same bedbugs," Morwenna said. Genevieve giggled. Morwenna kissed her once again and left her, cuddling her teddy bear.

She hesitated and looked out the window from the upstairs hallway. She could see that Shayne had bundled up and was headed to the garage. About ten feet behind him, someone else was walking. Too broad shouldered to be Bobby; it was Gabe. Gabe Lange was going out to help him.

Something stirred inside her.

Distrust. Sadly, she had a lot of her father inside her. She didn't naturally trust anyone. And they found him in the snow. He claimed to be a cop, but he hadn't been wearing any kind of uniform, and they'd found him with no identification. Was he who he said he was?

All she knew at that moment was that the guy

was following her brother. On a dark, snow-swept night. They were heading into the garage.

She tore down the stairs, pausing at the hooks by the door for her coat and scarf. Her brother was likely lost in his own thoughts as he always was, unable to feel the first hint of danger.

Luke DeFeo shivered, staring at a cottage that sat on the side of the mountain. It was dark, but everything was dark. Still, he had the feeling that there was no one there.

He swore aloud in the night. The air was bitterly cold, and he could feel it. He wanted to be off the damn frigid mountains, but there seemed to be no traffic anywhere in the area, and he had yet to stumble onto any signs that life actually existed in the frozen wasteland. He cursed Gabe in his mind; this was one hell of a way to spend the night.

He'd thought he'd killed him; he'd thought that he'd killed Gabe, but he hadn't. The deadly game between them was still on. Luke could somehow sense that Gabe was still out there.

Well, he didn't have to sense it, not really. Stumbling around in the snow and ice-covered wilderness, he had come upon the place where they had fought—and Gabe had been gone. So he was still out there, somewhere in the night.

Luke made his way to the little wooden cottage on the mountain. It was dark and he couldn't hear any signs of life. He rapped at the door and received no answer. After a moment, he threw his shoulder against the door, and then kicked it in. He stepped into the house, but as he did so, he knew that it was empty. The inhabitants were apparently smart—they'd gone somewhere for the holiday.

He looked around, and wondered if he wanted something from the cottage. But there wasn't anything there; it was empty and it was cold. It was a shelter against the cold and the snow and the wretchedness of the night, of course.

But he couldn't stay.

He hadn't killed Gabe.

He left the door to the cottage swinging and

started out, feeling the bitter cold again. He could take it.

He was going to find Gabe, and end the game between them.

Chapter 4

"I'm going to head out and help Shayne," Bobby told his mother. He'd come from the kitchen, having insisted he clean up the hot-cocoa cups. Stacy had been straightening out the apron around the Christmas tree to ready it for Shayne's packages.

"You don't need to help, Bobby—Gabe went out behind him, and Morwenna went running out after him." She was staring at the tree as she spoke, but turned to smile at him. "You did a beautiful job with the ornaments, Bobby."

"It was easy. Dad did the lights. That's the pain in the ass, Mom."

She rolled her eyes. "Butt, Bobby. Pain in the butt. It's a nicer word." She stepped closer to the tree, studying one of the ornaments. It was the little angel or cherub he had pondered himself earlier.

He walked over to his mother, setting a hand on her shoulder. "That's pretty," he told her.

She smiled. "I think I told you the story that goes with this ornament, years ago."

"Did you?"

"It belonged to my great-great-grandmother."

"Mom, the house is almost two hundred years old. And half the stuff in it belonged to your great-great-grandmother."

"Ah, but this one was special! During the winter of 1864, a wounded Union soldier found himself running through the mountains, terrified, of course, about what might happen to him if he was captured by a Confederate guerrilla band. The commanders of the armies, both sides, were fairly honorable men, but sometimes the militiamen and

the guerrillas combing the mountains were fanat-
ics—not so much on the eastern front, but in the
west the men were often little more than common
murderers. Anyway, my great-great-grandmother
found him trying to seek shelter in the barn—the
garage now. And she couldn't let any wounded
man suffer, and took him in to nurse him. When
the menfolk in the family wanted to turn him
in, she said she just didn't give a damn about the
war, she cared about people. He got a fever, and
he was delirious, and when he woke up, he said
that she was his angel. His angel of mercy. He had
this little ornament to bring home as a gift for his
mother, but when he left, he said that his mother
would want the angel who had saved his life to
have the figure. He said that he prayed the angel
would look after her all her days. She lived to be
ninety-nine, so I guess the angel was looking after
her."

"Great story, Mom," Bobby said. She smiled.
And for that minute, Stacy looked almost like
a young girl again. She was his mother, but it
seemed that he could take a step back for a mo-

ment and take a look at her as a human being. He smiled inwardly, thinking she must have really been something at one time. He'd always known that his big sister was beautiful. And now he could recognize the fact that Morwenna had gotten her looks from their mother.

Kids seldom saw such things, but it was nice to realize—Stacy was still a pretty woman.

"The story gets better," she told him. "The Union soldier she saved went on to become a congressman from Massachusetts—and he helped fight to stop the punitive measures toward the postwar South." She touched the ornament tenderly. "When I was little, her daughter, my great-grandmother, used to tell me that angels did influence our lives, and that they helped us sometimes, when we didn't even know they were there. I like to believe that, Bobby."

"Sure, Mom." He gave her a hug. He marveled at his mother, and he had to wonder if people did come together for a reason. His mom was the ray of hope and light. His father was the doomsayer. They could both be right; Mike MacDougal had seen all the worst that man had to offer his fellow man. Stacy believed in the goodness that she felt prevailed among most people.

"They've been out there a while," Bobby said. "I think I'll help. Maybe there's a bicycle out there and those misfits are dropping all the pieces!" With a quick kiss on the cheek, he left her, striding to the door for his heavy coat.

The snow kept falling in huge, wet flakes and the wind blew hard. Morwenna felt as if she was battling a storm in the Antarctic as she made her way to the garage. When she reached the side door, it was a fight against the wind to open it. But she suddenly felt desperate; she could see through the four-paned little window that Gabe was standing close to her brother by the trunk of his car.

The door flew open, slamming against the wooden wall of the garage.

Both men looked toward her; Gabe hurried over, drawing her in and closing the door.

"Hey!" Shayne said. "What are you doing out here? It's freezing!"

"I, um, you were taking some time. I thought you might need help," Morwenna said. She felt a little ridiculous, and then not. They didn't know Gabe Lange.

"Oh, we were just talking," Shayne told her. "I was showing Gabe some of the things for the kids."

"And we were discussing the merits of live action versus video games," Gabe said. "Shayne's right—this one electronic thingy he got for Connor is great—it's a word game, teaches you how to spell, and what the definitions for the words are once they're found. And you win funny little cars with each correct answer—virtual cars."

"Will it work—does it have to be downloaded?" Morwenna asked. "I'm surprised we still have electricity. The cable is down, and none of the phones work."

"It's battery operated, and doesn't need any downloads, so Connor will be able to play with it no matter, tomorrow," Shayne said. "I have to admit, I think the kids had a great time tonight—without electronic devices."

"Who knew you'd make such a great Mr. Mean?" Morwenna said lightly.

Shayne half smiled. "It was fun. I really had fun."

"Do you write children's books?" Gabe asked her.

"No! Oh, Lord, no," Morwenna said. "I'm an executive at an ad agency in Manhattan."

"Yeah, I heard that. But, people may do one thing for a living, and another on the side. I thought that maybe you wrote for children on the side. And I take it that you draw a lot?" Gabe asked.

"Sure. Sometimes. I always loved to draw."

"Once upon a time you spent a lot more time just doodling," Shayne said.

"I can't. I mean, I don't really have the time. Not anymore. Now I spend a lot of time in meetings," Morwenna said.

"You should illustrate," Gabe said.

She hesitated. She could have explained that she had intended to, things hadn't quite gone in the direction she had intended. "I don't really have the time," she said simply. "I can come up with the creatures, but I'm not sure what they should be doing. A story needs a beginning, a middle and an end."

"But you could work with someone else, right?" Gabe asked her.

"Sure," she murmured. "Maybe in my retirement."

"I guess we all do what we need to do in life," Gabe said. "You're good. And it's obvious that you love it. Maybe take a sketch pad on your next vacation."

"This *is* my vacation," she said.

"Morwenna is mourning the fact that she's not in Cancún," Shayne told him.

"I am not! I chose to be here," Morwenna said.

Shayne laughed and brushed her cheek with his knuckles, teasing her as he had when they'd been in high school. "Sense of duty, right, sis? Her lover boy is off in Cancún, and she must be dying to know what he's up to."

"Shayne, please, it's a mature relationship," Morwenna said.

"Ah," Gabe said knowingly. "Like an open relationship?"

"No! Oh, for God's sake, please. It's possible to have a relationship in which people remain monogamous when they're apart," Morwenna said.

"Sure," Shayne said, turning away.

"It is!" Morwenna insisted.

"I was agreeing with you, Morwenna. I'm sorry—I didn't mean to hurt you. I was just teasing, really," Shayne said.

"You didn't hurt me," she protested. *A lie! She was worried; if it had been a really good relationship, wouldn't he have told the others just to be adults and have a good time on their own because he wanted to be with the woman he loved at Christmas?*

Or were their values simply different? she wondered. It was hard to admit; she had come because of a sense of duty. But she had also wanted to come—Christmas to her had always been this house on top of the mountain. New Year's might be right for a wild jaunt, but Christmas meant being with the ones she loved. That didn't negate other values, she assured herself. It was just what it meant to her.

"I'm not a family member, but I'm glad that you're here," Gabe told her. "It's been nice to meet you."

She gave him a weak smile. *Really? I'd have thought about leaving you in the snow; I'm my father's daughter, braving the trenches of Manhattan in a state of continual suspicion.*

She wasn't sure what to reply.

"Well, you made a great Christmas elf," she told him.

"I'm going to haul in the first bag of stuff," Shayne said. He grimaced. "We were talking about putting the bicycle together out here...keep all the packing and stuff out of the house," he said.

"We were just about to start, and I'm afraid the reality may be as hard as the imagery we were playing with before," Gabe said.

"I'm good with directions. I'll help," Morwenna said.

"Okay, you two get started. I'll be right back. Or as soon as the wind will let me," Shayne told them.

Gabe got the door so Shayne could head out with a large canvas bag. She saw that the box with the bike parts was already on the floor, opened. "Where are the directions?" she asked Gabe.

"Right here," he said, handing her a sheet from the top of the box.

"Easy. A1 goes to A2, as soon as you have B1 connected to C1, and then, somehow, D2 has been thrown into the lot. Ah, there's E3!"

Gabe groaned, and started pulling all the pieces out of the box. They knelt down together to study the diagram.

Morwenna couldn't help but be aware of him as a man, and she found herself wondering how she would have felt about him if they'd met under different circumstances. But, of course, this *was* a strange circumstance, and she was committed.

She had never been able to date casually. Of course, she'd dated Alex before they'd become a couple, and she'd found it awkward and difficult. Her friends in Manhattan had tried hard to teach her that every dinner didn't have to lead to sex, and that she wasn't obligated to have sex, but then again, didn't she want it now and then? In college, she'd had one relationship, and they had both been honest and committed, and then, at graduation, they had realized the bond wasn't strong enough for either of them to change their goals in life, and they had parted as friends. And eventually, of course, their calls had grown infrequent, and time had gone by.

Then, Alex had come into the firm, and the first time they'd gone out, she'd been smitten. She'd still held back until they'd been seeing each other for a few months, and the time had been right, and she'd believed that they both really cared about each other. She had to admit to herself, though, that they hadn't used the all-important four-letter word yet—love.

"Hand over A1 there, will you?" Gabe asked. "The body of the beast!"

She did so.

"Your brothers are really good guys," he told her.

"Love them to pieces," she said. "I just wish that…"

He looked up at her. "What?"

Morwenna looked back at him for a moment, wondering how he managed to make them all talk about things that they wouldn't share often. With each other. With anyone. If they spoke to each other, they fought. And they weren't really into airing private grievances with others.

She laughed suddenly. "You're reminding me of how it was when we were kids. I could be ready to throttle Shayne or Bobby, but if anyone else said something about them, I'd be ready to throttle that person."

Gabe grinned. "I guess that's the way it should be."

"I think that Shayne's current situation is just terribly painful. He really loved Cindy. I don't think he was a great husband. I mean, he's so dedicated to his patients. Oh, he adores his kids, but Cindy was the one who was with them most, and I think he's as happy as can be that he does have them for Christmas, but without Mom and Dad or Cindy, I don't think he remembers how to do Christmas."

Gabe found the "screwdriver included!" bag and nodded as he divided his attention between her and his task. "The most intelligent people in the world can usually look around and figure out what would fix things for someone else, and yet struggle with their own situation," he said.

"Genevieve broke my heart tonight. In her prayers, she basically asked God to put her parents back together."

"That's natural."

"And probably impossible. Cindy, I'm sure, thought long and hard before she left my brother."

"Nothing is impossible while we're drawing breath, kid," he said lightly.

"Then you believe in miracles, huh?" Morwenna asked him.

"If you think about it, life itself is a miracle. Sure, I believe in miracles." He grinned at her, pausing for a moment. "Just like your little play—miracles are out there. We have to make them happen."

"Well, you're just like Little Miss Sunshine, Pollyanna and a ray of light, all rolled into one,"

Morwenna said. "Life isn't like that. It's all messy, and complicated, and I'm sure that Shayne tried to fix things. Sometimes, when things are broken, they're shattered, and that's that."

He laughed and sat back for a moment, staring at her. "Wow! From what I can see, you all have a really good life going here. The three of you grew up with parents who really love you. They have their personalities and their opinions, but they love you, and it's obvious that every move they've ever made was with your best interests at heart. Shayne is doing what he loves for a living. You have a good job, even if it's not what you planned, and if you had any balls, you would do what you really wanted. Your problem with the fellow your brother referred to as lover boy or boy toy is probably the fact that you decided you needed *someone,* even if he wasn't the right one, and you're really not happy with yourself, so you're playing the game of trying to assemble the right pieces. Bobby—"

"Yeah, go on, pick on Bobby, the dropout!"

Morwenna said, angry and about to get to her feet and leave.

"I was about to say that Bobby is the one on the right track. He knows what he wants—and he's going to go after it. His biggest fear is hurting those who love him while he's on the way. All that he needs is a little faith."

Morwenna frowned. "What are you talking about?"

"Your brother really is a brilliant musician. Have you ever really listened to him play? He's amazing. He wants to pursue it. But in your family music is a hobby. Bobby can make more out of it, he just feels he has to prove to all of you that he can do it before he really gives it his whole heart. But he's moving in the right direction."

"Well, thank you, Mr. Cop-without-a-badge-or-uniform!" Morwenna said. "And how do I fix my life?"

"Oh, Morwenna, that's so easy. Quit playing the game. Stop trying to fix other people, and support them, in whatever they need. Don't try to play any roles in life, and stop and think about what you really want," he told her.

"So simple!" she told him with heat. "So simple—and maybe you might want to think about life that way yourself! You're just great at pointing out problems. Surely you have something in your life that you're not dealing with. Maybe you should worry about yourself."

"I didn't mean to be intrusive," he said. "You're just good people—you should be happy."

"What is happy? I mean, who is happy every single minute?"

"Content, then. Happiness is going through life with problems, and yet knowing where you're going, and enjoying the moments that are filled with laughter and love."

I am *happy!* she thought defensively.

Was she?

She turned away from him. This time of year, getting together—it *could* be one of those times when they were just happy, and appreciating one another.

"Hey," he said softly, and she looked up at him.

For a moment, she felt as if the fleeting seconds of time they shared, on the floor in the cold of the garage, were some of the most intimate she had ever known. His eyes were a green like the grass in summer. They seemed to speak in a whisper to her soul. She wanted to touch his face, and marvel that anything with such rugged appeal could be so tender and knowing.

She almost moved back. She liked him. And she was in a relationship, and she wasn't going to have any dreams about a stranger suddenly cast on their doorstep.

"I'm sorry," he said. "I can see that you all wind up in tangles because you do love one another so much. But here's the good—whether or not there is a miracle and Cindy and Shayne wind up back together or not, they're on their way to being the best they can possibly be. Cindy sent those kids here, right? Likely because she decided that they should have a real family Christmas, even if that meant it was one without her."

Morwenna sighed. "Shayne thinks she wanted quality time with the new love of her life."

"Well, of course he does. Someday he'll step back and rethink that."

"What's this about Bobby? He's my brother—what do you think you know about him that I don't?" Morwenna demanded.

"You should ask Bobby," he told her. "Hand me part D3a, will you, please?"

She did so. For a moment, she didn't really see him. She rose awkwardly, thinking about the things Gabe had told her. It was true; Shayne was hurting. And Bobby...

She wanted to talk to her brother. Alone.

"There we go!" Gabe said.

Startled, she looked back to him. He had risen as well; the bike was completely assembled.

"Wow," she said.

He grinned. "Not bad, eh?"

"Not bad at all. Now, all we have to do is get it to the house in this storm."

As she spoke, the garage door opened with a thud. Bobby, bracing himself, stood in the doorway.

"Thank the Lord! It's done, and I don't have to help," he said, eyeing the bike.

"That's the ticket," Morwenna said. She smiled at her younger brother. "Get here as soon as it's done. But you can help. We have to get the bike up to the house. Where is Shayne? I thought he was coming right back?"

"Connor called him from upstairs—he wanted a glass of water. And maybe he still believes in Santa, just a little, because he didn't want to come down the stairs—maybe jinx the possibility," Bobby said. "Shayne's with him now."

"Good for them both," Morwenna said, her voice a little husky. She realized that she was fighting the desire to cry. They did have their health. They had each other. People, good people, were out of work, starving in America and around the world.

She walked over to her brother and gave him a fierce hug. "I love you, Bobby." Then she hurried out of the garage and headed for the house.

Despite the cold and the wind, she paused. The bright lights of the Christmas tree shone out on the crystal-white glitter of the snow. It was beautiful. The warmth inside beckoned to her.

Life itself was a miracle.

And the beauty of the night, even in the wind and snow, was astounding. She smiled to herself, thoughts swirling in a real prayer.

Happy birthday, Jesus. And thank you.

"Easier said than done!" Bobby laughed. He had the back half of the bike; Gabe had the front. It wasn't even that big a bike; it was just awkward making their way through the snowdrifts to the house. When they reached the door, though, Morwenna was waiting, and they were able to walk right in, shedding snowflakes as they did so. Bobby stared at Morwenna, feeling awkward for a moment. He smiled at her.

She smiled back.

Shayne came down the stairs just as they entered.

"Hey! Great. That's amazing! It's already together!"

"Your sister reads directions well," Gabe said.

"Let's put that right here, to the left of the tree," Stacy suggested. "Shayne, you did a great job getting stuff here at the last minute for the children."

"Thanks," he said huskily. "Too bad I can't give them the one thing they really want."

"No, not Cindy," Morwenna said, walking over to Shayne. She stood on her toes and gave him a kiss on the cheek. "But they've got their dad, and you're a great dad, Shayne."

"I suck," Shayne admitted.

"But you're already working on not sucking," Bobby said. "So all is good! Mom, the tree looks great. Absolutely great."

"I just have to sneak up to my room when I'm sure Genevieve is deep asleep to get a few more things," Morwenna said. "I have a little dress-up set I'd bought for Alex's niece and a comic-book creature one of our clients gave me. My real gifts for the kids went through Cindy, of course, but they'll have something from me."

"I scrounged together a few old pieces, too," Stacy said. "They'll be good."

"Well, I didn't scrounge anything, but I have a

Christmas-morning present for them, too," Bobby told them. He grimaced. "I wrote them a song."

"Their own song. Cool, really cool," Gabe said.

Mike MacDougal studied his son. "That will be great, Bobby. We'll all look forward to hearing it."

Bobby thought that his father sounded a little awkward; words of praise had always been hard for him. He smiled.

Stacy stretched and yawned. "Well, I'm to bed," she said. "It's been a wonderful Christmas Eve. Thank you all. Thank you all for being here with us."

Stacy walked over and kissed Morwenna, then Shayne, and then came to Bobby. There was something glittering in his mother's eyes.

Happiness, he thought.

He hugged her warmly in return. "Good night, Mom," he told her. "Thank you. It was a great Christmas Eve dinner."

"Glad you liked it," she told him. She turned, and paused, seeing Gabe. Stacy smiled warmly and gave him a hug as well. "Welcome to our home for Christmas. You're all set, right?"

"Your family has been great. I have more than I would have had anywhere," he assured her.

"Well, good night, kids," Mike said. He repeated Stacy's actions, giving each of his children a hug, and pausing in front of Gabe. He offered him a handshake. "Merry almost Christmas, Mr. Lange."

"And to you, sir," Gabe said.

Mike stared at him. "Aren't you worried? Your, uh, your prisoner is still out there—at large nearby."

"I will be vigilant," Gabe said. "I won't let any harm come to your family."

Mike wagged a finger at Gabe. "Trust me. *I* won't let any harm come to my family."

As his parents walked up the stairs, Bobby heard his father whispering to his mother. "What do we know? The guy could be a crook! We could wake up to find out that he's robbed the entire place. Or worse, we could *not* get to wake up at all!"

"Hush!" Stacy said.

But Mike raised his voice, intending to be heard.

"You know I always sleep with that shotgun by my bed. You never know when a starving bear is going to wake up."

"Bears hibernate, Mike, you know that," Stacy said.

Then they were upstairs and out of earshot. The three MacDougal children looked awkwardly at Gabe.

"Dad's been a prosecutor for a really long time," Bobby said.

Gabe laughed. "Hey, he's a bright man, and he's seen the worst. That's okay. It's not a bad thing to be prepared for—bad things."

"Yes, despite all the miracles in the world," Morwenna said, "they do happen!"

"So do good things," Gabe countered. As he spoke, the old grandfather clock in the parlor chimed midnight.

They all stood still, listening.

"Merry Christmas, bros!" Morwenna said then, and kissed Shayne and Bobby. She studied her brothers' expressions. "Merry Christmas," she said again softly. "And I hope that your present is the future, and that it brings you all that you want—and deserve," she said. She moved quickly away, and walked over to Gabe.

She hesitated a minute, and then gave him a hug. "And you'd better not prove to be a lowlife thief or anything of the like," she told him.

She turned around to look at them all. "I'm going to grab those little gifts for the kids. And, then, I'm cuddling up with my niece to get some sleep. See you all in the morning."

She ran up the stairs. Shayne, Gabe and Bobby called after her, "Merry Christmas!"

They looked at one another. "I'm going to go on up and cuddle with my son, myself," Shayne said. "Guess I need to grab those chances when I get them," he said.

"'Night, Shayne," Bobby said.

Shayne paused in front of Gabe. "Merry Christmas. And thanks."

"Hey, I need to thank you all," Gabe told him.

Shayne nodded and headed on up.

"Top bunk or bottom?" Bobby asked Gabe.

"Whichever one you don't sleep in," Gabe said. "I could be dying of hypothermia right now. Or resting on a slab at the morgue. I'm delighted just to be indoors."

"Actually, we're lucky we found you. It's been a helluva good Christmas Eve with you around, stranger. Glad to have you," Bobby told him.

And it was true. What might have been tedious had been fun; what could have been arguments had turned to camaraderie and laughter.

He found himself turning to the tree. One of the golden glowing lights was touching the face of the little angel ornament.

An injured cop had turned out to be their Christmas angel, in his way.

"Want some water or anything before I turn out the lights down here? It won't be completely dark. We leave the tree lights on through the night. My mom used to say they were a beacon for Santa. And, of course, since we burned logs in the fireplace, she convinced us that Santa had a key."

Gabe laughed. "Nope, I'm good. Thanks. I'll

head on up. Which did you prefer? The upper bunk, or the lower?"

"Top—but I really don't care."

"I'll crawl into the lower," Gabe said.

Bobby started around the house to check the doors and turn off the lights. When he returned to the parlor, he saw that Morwenna had set her extra gifts under the tree for the kids.

She was just walking back up the stairs.

"'Night, sis!"

"'Night!" she called back.

As she reached the upper landing, Gabe was just coming out of Shayne's room. Shayne must have supplied him with the flannel night trousers he was wearing.

Gabe and Morwenna almost ran into each other. Gabe was still shirtless, carrying the pajama top in his hands.

Morwenna seemed to have frozen there.

As had Gabe.

Bobby grinned.

Two such beautiful people; Morwenna in a long white

flannel gown, raven hair flowing down her back; Gabe,
appearing to have such strength.

"'Night!" Morwenna said, the sound almost desperate. She turned and fled into her own room.

"Good night," Gabe called after her.

Bobby grinned as he walked up the stairs. He thought that Morwenna had a bit of a crush on their visitor—and that the feelings were returned.

Gabe had already turned into the room. When Bobby entered, their visitor was in the lower bunk.

"Merry Christmas," Bobby said, crawling up.

"Yes," Gabe said thoughtfully. "Merry Christmas."

Bobby yawned. For a moment, he thought that if their visitor was a maniacal killer, he'd be the first to go.

But the guy wasn't a killer of any kind. He was certain. He didn't know how he was certain.

But, as the stranger seemed to be teaching them, sometimes, you just had to have faith.

Chapter 5

Morwenna woke up with a start. She could actually hear bells; church bells coming from the little village that was around the bend and down the mountain about a mile.

She started to move and realized that something warm was next to her, and she raised her arms quickly, hoping that she hadn't batted her niece in the head. She looked down at Genevieve, still sleeping soundly, little cheeks rosy and flushed.

She looked like an angel.

It had been nice sleeping with her; nice to wake up with a trusting little bundle of a child next to her. She rose carefully, trying not to awaken Genevieve, moved to gather fresh clothing as silently as she could and then headed into her bathroom to shower. As she turned on the water, she thought back to early yesterday morning, when she and Alex had stood in the shower together. They had teased and played, and it had been nice, and of course, he'd reminded her that she could still get on the plane with him—no matter what it cost, they could buy a ticket. She'd reminded him that he could forget Cancún and come with her.

But they'd parted anyway. He hadn't let her drive him to the airport; they were all going on one plane out of Kennedy, he told her, and Kennedy would be in the opposite direction. He wished her a wonderful Christmas, and sounded sincere when he said that she should enjoy her family.

She hoped she had sounded equally sincere when she had told him to enjoy Cancún.

Just a little more than twenty-four hours ago now and yet it seemed like forever.

As she stood under the warm spray of the shower, she wondered how her life in Manhattan could seem so far away. There had actually been moments when she hadn't really thought about Alex in Cancún, or really worried half as much as she might have. Well, that was probably thanks to the stranger, too; he seemed to be keeping them all on their good behavior.

And, apparently, he *wasn't* a maniacal serial killer, since she was pretty sure they'd all wakened that morning in their beds.

Dressed and ready for the day, she stepped back into her room. Genevieve was still sleeping.

Morwenna hesitated, and then quietly opened her bag. There was a wrapped gift there in her luggage, one she had forgotten to give Alex. She'd planned it as part of his Christmas stocking if he'd come home with her, since at the MacDougal house, everyone got a stocking.

It was a little box of her favorite men's cologne. She studied the prettily wrapped little package.

She honestly didn't even know if Alex liked it or not. He'd said he did when they'd started dating. But then, at that time, if she liked something, he liked it.

It was cologne, she could replace it easily. She found a new tag and put Gabe's name on it, and the words *From Santa*.

Morwenna left the room and hurried downstairs.

There was no one in the parlor as she dropped the little gift under the tree, or in the dining room. Her mother, she knew, was up. But as she headed for the kitchen, she paused. She could hear her mother speaking to Gabe Lange.

"It's my favorite day. My favorite day of the year. It always has been. I like my birthday just fine, mind you. Thanksgiving is wonderful, and so is Easter. But Christmas...I don't know. I always believe just a little in magic when it's Christmas Day," Stacy said.

"It's a lovely day," Gabe replied.

She started to move on in, but then hesitated; her mother spoke again, bringing up her name.

"I wish I could give that magic to my children," she said. "Morwenna..."

Morwenna tensed.

Eavesdropping was not at all nice! she reminded herself.

But she felt frozen in place.

"My daughter," Stacy continued, "I love her so much. And I don't know what happened. I think she forgot how to be happy. I think she even thinks she *is* happy most of the time, but...take a look at my husband. He's a rather suspicious fellow. Well, his father wanted him to be an attorney. I don't think he even liked the law at first—he went into the law because that's what the sons in the family did. Then, along the way, he discovered that he did have a passion for seeing that *victims* received what was right, and that those who hurt others must be put away. He did what people thought he should, but somehow he made it work on his terms. He seems gruff and hard sometimes, but when he wins a case and comes home having put away the bad guy, he's so happy! You're in law enforcement—you must understand some of the feelings he has, and how he can be up and down and frustrated. And when he doesn't win, I'm there to help him through the struggle. But with Morwenna...I fear sometimes that we hurt her. She's like a little hamster on a wheel, running and running. I worry that she's not going where she wants to be. Last night really brought it home to me. She's forgotten—and I think that most of the world forgets—that it's nice sometimes just to wake up and be happy for what we do have, and remember that *happy* isn't a constant state for anyone"

"Well, Mrs. MacDougal, I think you are wise beyond measure," Gabe told her. "And, to be truthful, I think that your daughter is very smart, and a very good person, and that she will find her way."

"Wenna!"

She turned, her cheeks reddening as she heard the whisper from the dining room doorway.

Bobby was there. He had pure mischief in his eyes and he shook his finger in a "no-no" gesture.

He tiptoed up to her. "Eavesdropping? On your mother?"

She elbowed him in the ribs. "I wasn't eaves-dropping!" she protested. "I just got here."

"Yeah, and you always walk around with your ear glued to the wall," Bobby said.

She elbowed him again. "Hey! Lay off the ribs, will you? There could be a hot girl in my future somewhere," he told her.

"Your future here? In this house?" she asked skeptically.

"No. But, my dear, just because the weather *was* so wretched we couldn't get out of the house and our little area, things always change! If the weather holds, we'll go down to the village. Gabe can get ahold of his headquarters and tell them that a con is running around somewhere, and we'll have a wassail drink at the old tavern later on. I think Mom wants to go to the cemetery and do her prayer thing there, and, of course, there's church tonight," Bobby reminded her.

"Ah, yes! Drive-in Mass."

"Gotta love Father Donaldson. He says that if he

can get his parishioners into the church for twenty minutes and a quickie mass, it's better than no mass at all."

"Which works for Dad," Morwenna agreed. "I think Mom would like a service with more singing, and a sermon that's longer than 'Please, Lord, help team X win the Super Bowl!'"

"I think that Mom is just glad Dad goes to church, and agrees to her little MacDougal prayer service at the cemetery," Bobby said.

"You're probably right," Morwenna said.

Stacy came through the swinging door, smiling. "I thought I heard you two out here. Good morning. Good—beautiful—Christmas morning!"

Gabe followed her out of the kitchen, smiling to see them. Morwenna caught his smile—Lord, but it was a good smile. But he wasn't just a stranger, she reminded herself, there was something about him that made the odd little sensual twinges she was feeling seem just not right somehow.

Didn't matter! Soon she'd be back in Manhattan, running the rat race and spending time with Alex.

"Merry Christmas," he said.

"And likewise!" she returned. "You slept well?"

"Like a baby."

As Gabe replied, Morwenna's father came into the dining room. "Merry Christmas, all. The little ones up yet?"

"Genevieve was still sleeping when I got up," Morwenna said.

"Well," Mike said, "I imagine they'll be up soon enough. Is coffee on in the kitchen?"

"Yes, dear, I'll get you a cup," Stacy said.

But Mike MacDougal set his hands on his wife's shoulders and kissed the top of her head. "Thank you, Stacy. I can get coffee. You spoil us all."

"I'll take some, too, Dad," Bobby said.

"You can come in and fix your own coffee. I don't know what you take with it these days," Mike said.

As Mike disappeared into the kitchen, they heard a loud screech of delight from the parlor.

"Kids are up!" Stacy said happily, hurrying out.

Morwenna followed her mother. She paused though, in the doorway, her smile deepening, something tugging at her heart.

Connor and little Genevieve were in front of the tree, hand in hand, staring at the ornaments and the packages beneath. Connor had let out the whoop, having seen his new bicycle.

"Santa came—I told you he would come," Genevieve said.

Shayne had followed his children down the stairs and stood behind them, silent. Connor turned around and hurried over to him, throwing his arms around his father. "Thanks, Dad," he said huskily. "It was the only...like, *thing* that I wanted and kind of needed."

Morwenna felt her heart would break as she watched her brother put his hand gently on his son's head. "I'm afraid you won't be able to use it much for a while. I'm pretty sure the snow is piled high in Pittsburgh, too. And don't worry— you don't have to keep it at my apartment. You can keep it at your mom's house. You go back and forth from school there most of the time."

Connor nodded. "Thanks," he said again.

"Daddy, can I open something, please?" Genevieve asked. "Connor can see his bike! My stuff is all wrapped," she said.

"Ask your grandmother. She's our mistress of ceremonies," Shayne said.

Genevieve looked hopefully to her grandmother. "Go for it, Genevieve. In fact, why don't you and Connor hand out the presents. Hand them all to everyone first, and then we'll open in order of our ages, youngest to oldest."

Genevieve giggled. "That means me first!"

"And Connor second."

"Anyone else for coffee or cocoa?" Morwenna asked. "I can make it while Genevieve is handing out the gifts."

"I'll help you," Gabe said. He shrugged. "I'm not a family member—I can give out coffee and keep the kitchen going, and I'll enjoy watching all of you in between."

"You may be surprised," she told him. "But sure, help me hand out coffee."

Genevieve and Connor were already out by the tree, looking for names on tags.

Morwenna smiled as Gabe followed her into the

kitchen. As she poured coffee into mugs, Gabe got the milk from the refrigerator and found a copper-bottomed pan hanging from the wooden overhead above the workstation in the center of the kitchen.

"Why don't I heat up the milk for the cocoa?" he said.

Morwenna went for the sugar, and looked over at Gabe. "This fellow that you were chasing—what had he done?" she asked.

"Luke DeFeo? He's been sentenced before—petty larceny. This time he stole the funds for the homeless from a church just outside Richmond."

"A thief, but not a murderer?" Morwenna asked. "Well, that's good to know, if this guy is running around the mountain somewhere."

"Not a murderer; but still a very dangerous man," Gabe said. He hesitated, adding the chocolate squares Morwenna provided to the heating milk. "Sometime this evening, thanks to your brother's kind medical care, I'll be able to head out and try to track him again. I really need to find him before the day is done."

"Why? What difference will it make when you catch him?" Morwenna asked.

Gabe looked at the milk and chocolate he was stirring. "Because he's especially dangerous on a day like today, that's why." He looked at her.

There was something about his words that seemed strange.

"Yes, I guess, what with all the presents. But I'm not sure you should head back out into the snow today," she said. "You seem to be absolutely fine, but you did take a nasty beating yesterday."

"I'll be fine," he assured her.

She realized that she didn't want their uninvited guest to leave.

"Gabe, we are the citizens you're supposed to be protecting, no matter the actual jurisdiction. If you're looking for someone who might be interested in stealing, you should hang with us most of the day."

"I will protect you from him," Gabe said, his tone almost fierce.

"I believe you will," Morwenna said. She felt awkward for a moment. "Mom likes to do a lit-

tle service at the cemetery, and then we're heading down to the village tavern for a drink. And
hey, we need some outside company, to divert us
from ripping on each other," she said. "Kind of
sad, isn't it? Most of us really love our families so
much, and yet, we're cruel to one another in a way
we wouldn't be with others. I guess that's because
others would just walk away."

"That's one way to look at it," he told her.
"Maybe, sometimes, we're mean to our families
because they're the people who see what we don't
want to admit to ourselves, and will love us no
matter what."

"I think I'm just going to call you Mr. Sunshine
from now on," Morwenna told him.

He laughed, stirring the hot chocolate mixture
a last time. "Doesn't that have to do with the fact
that you can see the glass as half-empty—or half-
full?"

"Come along, Mr. Sunshine. The gifts are surely
divided by now," Morwenna said.

They made two trips with the cups of hot chocolate and coffee, and then took seats on the sofa

where their presents had been left. Morwenna quickly saw that she wasn't the only one who had found something for Gabe; he had a stack of four gifts.

He looked around the room. "You didn't need to do this! You gave me everything—by taking me in," he said.

Genevieve came to him and with her little hands pushed him down into his chair. "Santa knew you were here, Gabe. But I get to go first!"

Morwenna noted that her mother had done a good job whipping up stockings for the children at the last minute. Genevieve received Fruit Roll-ups, quarters for the games at the tavern and a pretty little set of silver earrings—probably something her mom had bought for herself, since she was always losing one earring. She was delighted. Her present from her father was a real working kids' stove and an electronic game. Stacy had wrapped up one of her collectible Cabbage Patch dolls, and the little girl was in awe of it, playing with it as Connor opened the rest of his gifts.

Then Bobby told them that his gift was a song, and he pulled out his guitar and sang to them:

> *Christmas morning, what a thrill, for Gen and Connor are here,*
> *Pretty girl, handsome lad,*
> *Giving us the best Christmas ever had!*
> *Christmas Day, what a thrill, for Gen and Connor here!*
> *Clever girl, brilliant lad,*
> *When they're around, nothing can be bad,*
> *Oh, it's a Gen and Connor Christmas,*
> *How we love it, ever so dear,*
> *Connor and Genevieve,*
> *Ring the bells!*
> *Light the lights!*
> *When Gen smiles, all the world is bright!*
> *Ring the bells!*
> *Light the lights!*
> *When Connor is with us,*
> *The world is all right!*
> *Oh, it's a Gen and Connor Christmas,*
> *A Gen and Connor Christmas,*

And Christmas Day
Burns so bright!

The kids, giggling all the while, pounced on Bobby, hugging him.

"Hey," Bobby cried. "Munchkins! Watch the guitar."

"Come on, Uncle Bobby. You're up next!" Genevieve told him.

"Okay, okay. Pummel the flesh, but not the guitar, eh?" Bobby teased. "Gen, you help me with that one. I don't wrap well, and I open even worse."

"You can't open a present badly," Genevieve told him, but she began tearing at the wrapping paper for him.

Bobby was also delighted with his gifts. His stocking had been filled with Pez animals, beef jerky, turkey jerky and more. His parents had gotten him a new, down-lined coat. Shayne had gotten him an electronic reader with a special music application, and Morwenna had gone out of her way wrapping up a gift certificate to a national-chain music store, nestled in a bed of guitar picks, strings and a tuner.

"Now you, Auntie Wenna!" Genevieve said. "Are you really bad at unwrapping, too?"

"Well, of course I am," Morwenna said, sitting her niece on her lap. "Go for it, girl."

First, the stocking. Morwenna's had sugar substitute, lip gloss guaranteed to prevent chapping in cold weather, nail polish and emery boards. Genevieve happily tore apart Morwenna's gifts for her. Morwenna oohed and aahed over her presents—a computer bag with just the right number of pockets, a beautiful black cocktail dress, a snow hat with matching gloves and a tiny little box.

"What's this?" Genevieve asked.

"I don't know. Open it."

Genevieve opened the little box. It held a delicate gold chain that held an angel or cherub, almost like the one on her mother's tree. It was a beautiful piece.

Morwenna looked around the room; there was no signature on the box.

"Mom, where did you find this?" Morwenna asked.

"I didn't. Mike?" Stacy asked.

"No, I didn't buy it, I'm sorry to say," Mike said.

"Not me—I'm the hat and gloves," Bobby said.

"I'm the computer bag," Shayne said.

"Santa Claus!" Genevieve announced.

"How curious," Morwenna said. She took out the chain and little medallion, and Bobby offered to fasten it around her neck. She felt it as it lay against her flesh, and touched it gently. "I'll figure out my secret Santa, guys. But thank you one and all."

"So who is next—Shayne or Gabe?" Connor asked.

"Gabe—I believe I'm older," Shayne said.

Gabe seemed humbled and appreciative as he opened his gifts. When he got to Morwenna's present, he smiled at her. "Uncanny! It's my favorite. But—"

"Hey!" Stacy said. "You're our guest. Please enjoy what little we have to offer. And, now, Shayne, it's to you!"

Shayne feigned excitement over his gifts and Morwenna wanted to make it all better for her older brother.

It was his first Christmas as a divorced man.

The kids went on to help Mike and Stacy open their presents, and then Stacy announced that it was time for a quick breakfast.

"But not too many people in the kitchen, please, or I can't get anything done," Stacy said. "Morwenna, you and Gabe can come with me. Bobby, you and Dad set the table. Shayne, gather up all the wrappings and get them into the garbage—all right, everyone?"

It was agreed. Stacy had her crowd well in hand; she turned on a Christmas CD, and everyone went about their tasks.

On egg duty with Gabe in the kitchen, Morwenna realized that he had put on a spray of the men's cologne she had given him.

She smiled. "Nice," she told him. She hesitated, staring at him. "Was the angel from you?"

"Angels are from above," he teased in return.

"But, seriously, was it? Was it meant for some-one else in your life?" she asked.

"Was the cologne?"

"Cologne is easy—it's in every department store," she said.

He laughed. "Maybe angels are easy, too, if you just look."

She turned away, humming to the song on the CD, "O Little Town of Bethlehem."

"You don't sound at all like a sick hyena," Gabe told her.

"Anyone can hum," she assured him.

"Watch the eggs!" Stacy commanded.

They both laughed. Once Stacy pulled the toast out and Morwenna's father and brothers wound up in the kitchen and they all bumped into each other as they brought the food out to the table.

In a few minutes breakfast was all set up, and they gathered around the table, and there were several minutes of "Pass the toast, please," or "Can you hand me that plate of hash browns?" until all their plates were filled. Coffee and drinks were poured and passed, and everyone praised Stacy for a delicious breakfast, and then Bobby told the kids to go up and get their snowsuits on, threatening them with a snowball fight.

When the kids had gone with Shayne to get dressed for the snow, Stacy sat back with her coffee and said, "Bobby, play us something. Something Christmasy and magical."

When Bobby returned with his guitar, he perched on a kitchen stool and strummed a few notes.

"'O Holy Night,'" Gabe suggested.

Bobby nodded and played and sang. When he finished, Stacy stood and came over and kissed him on the cheek, tears brimming in her eyes. "That was really beautiful," she said.

"I've applied to Juilliard," Bobby said, wincing slightly as he looked at his father. "I may well not make it. I don't know how many incredibly talented people apply every year. But I know how you feel, Dad, and you won't be responsible for helping me. I've found a way to work through school."

"Juilliard!" Stacy said.

"Juilliard," Mike repeated, frowning slightly, clearly taken off guard.

"Juilliard is one of the most prestigious schools in the country, Bobby. I hope you make it!" Morwenna said, surprising herself with her readiness to step in for her brother.

"I'll know in the next few days," Bobby said, sounding amazed by her enthusiasm. "I missed the usual auditions, and had to get a special audience with the music school, but somehow, believe it or not, they were chock-full of pianists and violinists, and a little light on those auditioning for guitar this year. So...I'll know right after New Year's."

"Juilliard," Mike said again. He blinked. "Bobby, do you know how hard it is to make a living with a guitar? Every kid out there has one. Every kid dreams of being a rock star."

"Might as well dream big," Bobby said. He glanced at his sister, silently thanking her for the support she had offered him.

"It's not just a 'rock star' thing, Dad," Morwenna said. "You just heard him play a Christmas carol that was so beautiful, it made tears spring to the eyes."

"It's a hard, hard living, son," Mike said.

"I don't mind working hard," Bobby said.

Morwenna glanced at Gabe; of course, he wasn't a member of their family, and he hadn't said a word. As she looked at him, though, she realized that he had known. Bobby had told him.

Mike stood. "We can talk about this later," he said.

Bobby stood as well. "We can talk all you want, Dad, but my mind is made up. I know you want the best for me, and I respect that. But if I don't make it into Juilliard, I'll find another music academy or institute. I'm going for what I want. I'm not going to be Morwenna, brilliant—and languishing in business meetings!"

"What?" Morwenna gasped. "Bobby, I have a great job—"

"Yes, you have a great job, and it should have given you a wonderful outlet for your work. But it didn't. It turned you into corporate America, which would be just fine, if what you really wanted was corporate America. You're not that old, Morwenna. Actually, that wouldn't even matter. You can start over at any time in life—you can start over and start drawing again. Anyway, sorry. I didn't want to ruin Christmas for anyone. I'm going to head out and have a snowball fight with the kids like I promised."

Indignant, Morwenna watched him go. She blinked hard; she had a great job. She might know herself that corporate America hadn't been her dream, but to the outside world, she had an enviable job. She had a great guy, Alex. This—this being home for the holidays—this was out of context.

She looked at her parents. They still seemed to be in shock.

Gabe stood up. "I think I'll join in the snowball fight," he said. He looked down at Morwenna and offered her a hand. "Are you coming?"

"Yes, I'm going to whack the sh—the stuffing out of Bobby," she said. She headed out quickly, and Gabe followed her. At the door she slipped into her heavy parka and gloves, and burst outside, gathering up a handful of snow before she reached the yard. Connor and Genevieve had been using one of the high-growing pines as shelter against Bobby's attacks. Morwenna headed straight for her brother with a big, wet, sloppy snowball.

She creamed him.

The kids, laughing delightedly, came from around the pines. Bobby was down in the snow, howling in protest and laughter, when Shayne came running out and pelted Morwenna. She stood, aimed back at him and hit Gabe in the chest.

In a few minutes, they were rolling in the snow, all soaked and still tossing snow and laughing.

Morwenna was vaguely aware of the crunch of footsteps on the snow; she was still startled when a deep, loud angry voice called out.

"Hey!"

They all paused, rolled and looked down the slope. A tall man in a Virginia State Police uniform and parka was heading up toward them.

"Hey!" he shouted again. "Stop right there, all of you. Don't move. You're harboring a *murderer!*"

Chapter 6

Stunned, half-frozen in the snow, Morwenna stared at the newcomer.

He was a tall, well-muscled man of about thirty, or thirty-five, dark-haired, with fierce dark eyes and a rugged-looking face.

He could have been a cop...

He was in uniform...

"Get up, Gabe!" he said, striding over to stand above Gabe, Morwenna and the kids where they were tangled together in their snow brawl.

Gabe stood, staring at the newcomer. "He isn't a cop," he said evenly. "He has the clothes because he stole them off me. He isn't a cop, and I'm not a murderer, and *he* isn't even a murderer."

Morwenna was vaguely aware that the door to their house had opened and closed.

Genevieve was clinging to her pants. Connor was just staring wide-eyed.

Shayne walked the few feet to the men. "All right, let's sort this out here," he said. "May I see your credentials? Are you armed?"

The man's eyes flickered for a minute, and then seemed to gleam with an angry fire. "My sidearm was lost when I grappled with this escaped convict. Trust me, he's dangerous. I need to take custody of him now."

"He's lying," Gabe said. "He's the convict. The thief."

The door to the house burst open and Mike, followed by Bobby, came bursting out of the house.

Mike had his shotgun, and it was aimed at the two strangers in their midst.

"All right, what the hell is going on here?" Mike demanded.

"I'm Officer Luke DeFeo of the Virginia State Police," the newcomer said, his voice filled with authority. "You've been deceived by a criminal, a convicted killer."

"That's a lie. He's the con. You found me half dead in the snow because we wrestled when I was trying to bring him back to justice. He stole my clothing, and gave me his," Gabe said. "You have to believe me. This man isn't a murderer, but he could prove to be the most dangerous man who ever walked into your lives."

"Don't be ridiculous! Put that gun down. You can see that I'm the cop!" Luke DeFeo said. He started walking toward Mike angrily.

But Assistant District Attorney Michael Mac-Dougal was no man's fool. Morwenna was proud when her father cocked the shotgun and said, "I have damn good aim. You stay right where you are. Now, can either of you prove what you're saying? Let's see some ID."

"Look at what I'm wearing!" DeFeo snapped.

"I can see what you're wearing," Mike said. "And you may well be a cop, but this fellow has been with us for a lot of hours now, and we're all alive and well, and it seems that things are appearing in our house rather than disappearing."

Morwenna felt the little angel against her neck. It wasn't studded with gems, but it was still a nice piece. He had given it to her.

Suspicion crept into her mind. Had he taken it off someone else? Maybe someone now lying dead in the snow.

"You leave him alone!" Genevieve said, leaping up with the agility of a child and running to DeFeo. She gave him a hard kick in the shin.

DeFeo let out an angry yell, and almost reached for Genevieve.

"My sister!" Connor cried.

"You touch my daughter, and I'll kill you, cop or no!" Shayne announced. "Genevieve, get over here."

Genevieve obeyed without a murmur.

"Connor, you, too," Shayne said.

Gabe and Morwenna stood, dusting snow from their bodies, staring, and watching and waiting.

"You're going to find yourself under arrest for aiding and abetting a criminal," DeFeo said.

"Let's see your credentials," Mike said firmly.

"Hey, you can see I have a badge."

"And I'll see some ID, too," Mike said firmly.

DeFeo scowled. "I don't have my wallet—I lost it in the tussle with the con you're protecting!"

"If you have no real ID, I have no real proof. No one is going to intimidate me," Mike announced. "If I know one thing, I know the law. And I know that we don't have any way of knowing which of you is telling the truth. So—you. Yeah, you, Virginia State policeman. Raise your arms. Bobby, see if he has cuffs. And if he does, put them on him."

"Yes, sir! Yes, sir, Dad!" Bobby said, and sprang into action.

Morwenna had never seen her brother Bobby as the tough-guy type, and then again, she'd never seen lifesaving Shayne threaten someone's life. But then, his children had been threatened, and now Bobby was ready to spring to the fore.

"If your son touches me, I'll see that he does jail time, too," DeFeo warned.

"And if you touch my son, I'll blow your head off," Mike promised.

Bobby walked straight for DeFeo. "Listen, buddy, if you're legit, and we all wind up at a police station looking like fools, we'll take our chances in court," he said.

"You're risking your lives!" DeFeo said, standing still as Bobby found the cuffs he did have hooked to his belt and slipped them around De-Feo's wrists. "I'm telling you, he's the criminal. If you hold me against my will, he'll find a way to kill me, and slaughter you and your whole family in your beds!"

"We're not taking any chances," Mike said. "We're not taking chances—with anyone. I'm going to disbelieve both of you—until we learn the truth. Morwenna, get in the house. I have good nylon rope in the pantry. I want Gabe tied up, too."

Morwenna stared back at her father, blinking.
"Morwenna!"

She looked down at Gabe, stunned to realize
that they really didn't know. If Gabe was a crook,
he could be damn good at deceiving people. It felt
as if the cold suddenly swept through her. *Why
wouldn't he have killed them last night?*

Because he'd wanted his turkey, that's why.

Gabe looked up and said calmly, "Get the rope,
like your father says. Keep us both tied up, and
away from the house. Keep your family safe."

"But, Daddy," Genevieve began.

"Hush," Shayne said softly.

"Connor, Genevieve, come with me, please,"
Morwenna said, and hurried into the house. Stacy
was standing in the parlor, looking out the window, her face knit in a worried frown.

"Morwenna?"

"That guy showed up, saying Gabe is a crook,
and that he himself is a cop," Morwenna explained
briefly.

"I was so worried when I saw your father get
the shotgun. I tried the phone again, but that and

the computer are still down, too. We've got electricity, but the television is all static. Morwenna, what are we going to do?"

"Keep them both tied up until we can get help," Morwenna said.

"We're on a mountaintop!" Stacy said.

"Mom, Dad has it covered. Besides, we have cars," Morwenna assured her.

Morwenna hurried back out, disturbed to see that her mother had come out to the front without even bothering to put on her coat. Though she had locked the door behind her, with the children inside.

She rushed by her, though. Gabe was standing a distance from Luke DeFeo. He offered his hands to her as she approached him.

"Behind his back!" DeFeo said. "Like you did me!"

"Wait!" Stacy said. She walked forward into the group. "One of these men is a criminal, and we really don't know what kind of criminal. But one of them isn't. And we're not breaking any arms or starving either of them. Tie their hands in front. We have the shotgun, and there are five of us adults here—we can watch them."

Shayne walked over to their mother. "Mom, we can't know how long until the phone and computer are back up, and it looks like we might have more bad weather coming in. We have to make sure that these guys are secure."

He pointed to the sky; it had been so blue.

Now, gray clouds were hovering. Strange gray clouds. Morwenna couldn't tell if they were coming from east or west, north or south. But they seemed to be converging over their house.

"We'll take turns watching them," Stacy insisted.

Gabe lifted his hands.

"Secure, Morwenna!" her father called.

"Yes, sir."

Gabe didn't move. She was close to him. The subtle scent of the cologne she had given him seemed to sweep around her. She looked at him. His eyes remained steady, green and open.

She looked down and tied his hand securely in a clove hitch. Her father, still keeping an eye on

Luke DeFeo as Bobby recinched the metal cuffs, walked over to see that she had tied the knot correctly. He nodded his approval.

"Now what?" DeFeo asked. He let out a sigh. His voice changed to something that was just weary. "This is ridiculous, honestly. You all need to help me. You seem like a nice family. I don't want you running into trouble. If you don't see what's going on here soon, you will face jail time, and you've just afforded yourselves a miserable day. You're going to spend your Christmas staring at the two of us. I would have taken this wretch back to justice!"

"And how were you going to do that?" Mike MacDougal asked him, his words barking. Morwenna imagined him in a courtroom. Her father, she knew, often managed to get people to say things they had surely never intended to say. "You came by foot."

"I'd have walked the bastard down the mountain," DeFeo said, his tone angry again. Then he seemed to gain control. "Look, you've all been fooled. You don't know what you're dealing with here."

"That's right," Shayne said quietly. "We don't know what we're dealing with here."

"And there's no way in hell anyone is walking anyone down the mountain," Stacy said. "It's a hard trip at best—hours walking in spring. There is weather coming in again."

"That's right, and you should let me handle it. We'll be out of your way in a moment," DeFeo pleaded.

"So…what now?" Morwenna asked.

Mike looked at the sky. "It may clear up soon enough," he said. "I can't tell right now exactly what the weather is going to do, but I think it would be foolhardy to try to reach even the village right now. Looks like we'll have to hold tight for a while."

"The garage and the shed," Stacy said. "You've got to keep them separated, and out of the wind. As soon as the weather clears, we'll get them both down to the tavern. They must have a way to reach some kind of help there."

"Bobby, you're on watch with Gabe. Shayne, you take DeFeo. The toolshed is empty. I brought the shovel and anything else anyone could use as a weapon into the house once we had a guest in the house," Mike said, glancing toward Gabe. "Shayne, you keep the shotgun. God knows what someone could find in the garage. I'll spell you in thirty minutes. Morwenna, you'll take over for Bobby."

Morwenna nodded. Neither of the men offered resistance as they were brought, handcuffed, to their respective places, Mike behind them both.

Morwenna looked up. The sky was darkening, and it couldn't have been later than ten in the morning.

As her father walked back to the house, he said, "I guess we'll have turkey later, Stacy. As soon as we can, we'll head down to Scott's Tavern with these two men."

Stacy started to walk into the house, and then she paused, looking at her husband. "The cemetery is on the way," she said.

"Stacy, we've got a criminal on our hands, and—depending on which man you believe—one of them might be a murderer."

Stacy straightened her shoulders. "The weather is going to be iffy all day. The cemetery is on the way to the village. It will only take a minute or two."

"Stacy," Mike said, "we could walk all the way and get rid of these two guys—"

"Mike! There's no guarantee that we'll have any communication when we reach the village, and no guarantee that there will be someone there who can watch them. This may remain our burden until we can get help up the mountain. The cemetery is on the way—we're going to stop briefly. We can keep the shotgun on them for one minute while we say a prayer. I'm still saying my Christmas prayers over my family's graves!"

With that, Stacy walked firmly into the house. Mike followed, but the door slammed in his face. He turned and looked at Morwenna and the kids. "All right, so the cemetery is on the way. How ridiculous is all this? One of us will stand with the shotgun trained on the two of them, and we'll say a prayer—in a graveyard. Christmas!"

He didn't say it, but Morwenna could almost imagine that he did.

Christmas! Bah, humbug!

"Look, I'm really sorry about this," Bobby said. And then, a little edge of doubt crept in. How often had he seen his father exhausted when a judge had ruled out key evidence and the jury was being swayed because the con could speak so persuasively?

Did he want to believe in this guy because this guy wanted him to believe in him?

"At least, I think I'm sorry," he muttered.

"It's all right. Man is a creature who must see something, hold it, find it tangible, before he really believes," Gabe said.

"He is wearing the uniform," Bobby pointed out.

"So he is."

Gabe walked ahead of Bobby into the shed.

There were two little windows in the small

building, so light could come in. When there was light. Right now, the sky was darkening. Bobby ushered Gabe in; even out of the growing wind, though, the shed was cold. The garage, he figured, was just as cold. But there were lights in the garage; several of them. The shed had one overhanging bulb. Bobby turned it on. It provided some light. A concrete floor had been poured years before, but the concrete emanated cold.

Gabe sat down against the back wall. There were wooden shelves and brackets, but, as his dad had said, the few tools they usually kept there had been brought into the house. His father, he realized, was a smart man.

"Bobby, there's nothing in this shed I could use to hurt anyone, if I had that in mind," Gabe said. "You don't have to stay out here—it's freezing."

"Yeah, it's cold," Bobby said briefly. "When Morwenna comes, I'll see to it that you get some blankets out here. And, hopefully, this won't last long. We'll get you both down to the tavern, or we'll get law enforcement up here one way or the other."

Gabe nodded. "Hard to tell. If a bad storm comes in…" He grinned. "Too bad you didn't bring your guitar. I'd be entertained. Honored, actually. And, at least you've said what you needed to say to your family now. You've got it in you."

Bobby laughed. "You want to know the funniest thing? I had confidence, and I had hope. But now that I've spit it all out, I'm suddenly afraid."

Gabe thought about that for a minute. "Well, before, if you failed, you were just failing yourself. Now, in your mind, if you were to fail, you'd be failing them instead."

"Failing everyone," Bobby murmured.

"Personally, I think the only way you fail is if you never try," Gabe said lightly.

Gabe seemed comfortable enough—he was shivering a little—but he seemed relaxed. *Resigned,* maybe. They might have been having a conversation in a warm kitchen over a cup of coffee.

But, Bobby thought, if he'd wanted to, Gabe could suddenly…

Head butt him?

"I'm telling you the truth," Gabe said, as if reading his mind. "I'm the cop—he's the bad guy."

"And I want to believe you," Bobby said.

"I'm glad."

"But I can't let you go."

"I know that. I understand."

"My mother, my sister…my niece and nephew… they are all vulnerable here," Bobby said.

"I know. I told you…I understand."

Bobby walked away from the door, looking up at the sky.

It seemed the darkness was closing in all around them, but in the center of it all, there was light. Maybe the weather would break.

He prayed heartily that it would do so…and soon.

Shayne leaned against his car, the shotgun in his hand as he stared at the man in the Virginia State Police uniform.

The guy wasn't fighting with him. He was just leaning against the garage, staring at him with a hard look that made his features severe.

"I wish you'd listen to me," DeFeo said at last. "You look like an intelligent guy. You can *see* that I'm a cop, no matter what kind of story that guy gave you. Look, he's got that green-eyed thing going for him. He knows how to say all the right things. That's how he managed to break out. He was being transferred from one facility to another, talked the guard into letting him have a cigarette—then bashed the poor fellow's head halfway in. You should be worried—that's your sister, I take it—and your mom. And your children. You've got a lot at stake here. Think about it. He's been using you."

"He could have killed us in our sleep last night or robbed the place blind," Shayne said. "He didn't."

DeFeo sighed. "Ted Bundy."

"What?"

"Ted Bundy. The serial killer. You know he actually babysat for his neighbor, right? John Wayne Gacy—he was a clown. Hey, kids love clowns. Don't you get it—the good-guy thing is an act."

"He's been acting well enough to win an Oscar,"

Shayne said. His voice was even. His pulse was racing. What if they were wrong? This guy did look and sound like a cop. And he had a badge—but he didn't have an ID.

Shayne felt a cold sweat break out.

His children... What if they had entertained some kind of real crook, a killer? What if Gabe Lange was just what this guy said he was, and DeFeo had come upon them just in time to save them?

"Officer DeFeo," he said, "you may be all that you say you are, but we don't know that any more than we know that he *isn't* who he claims to be. Just wait it out. When we can, we'll get to the authorities, and if we've wronged you, I'll apologize a thousand times over."

DeFeo shook his head, disgusted. "And what if he breaks out? Who is watching him next? Your sister, right? What if she falls for his act?"

"My sister isn't stupid."

"Not unless he talks her into being stupid. I'm sure he's given her all kinds of speeches on how wonderful she is at something, at how she needs to trust her instincts and have belief in herself and all that. That's his game. I know this guy—trust me," DeFeo said.

"She's not going to fall for any lines. She's in a relationship."

DeFeo laughed. "Sure. And he's making her doubt that relationship."

"This conversation is going nowhere," Shayne said. "I'm not letting you go."

"Just because your father is a fo—just because your father is misguided is no reason for you to wind up caught in the trap. You're taking a chance with your children. That's damn dangerous, my friend. I'm telling you, he's been using you. When he was done playing his game, when your mother had cooked everything up for a great turkey dinner, your family would have been done for. You really want to thank your lucky stars that I found this old house when I did."

"My father isn't a fool, DeFeo. He's done the one really smart thing—he's refused to take either of you at face value."

"Sure, that would be smart. If it weren't possible that Gabe would escape—and bring us all down, because I'm handcuffed and can't help you. Let's pray he doesn't get his hands on that shotgun, that's all I have to say."

Shayne didn't answer him. He couldn't help but listen to him, and he couldn't help but wonder if he was right.

DeFeo was silent for a while. "Cute kids," he said finally, as if he felt the need to talk about something.

"Yep."

"You here with them alone? Where's the wife? Oh, sorry, you're divorced, I take it."

"Yep."

"I've been down that path," DeFeo said. "I guess she was good to let you have them for Christmas. Usually, after a divorce, the mother has the power. Fathers are screwed. They pay all the bills, and the wives either hound them for more support, or play games, not even letting the dads see the kids."

"You're divorced?"

DeFeo nodded. "I spent hours working. She spent them at a gym. Took off with a personal trainer, and still got the kids. And I still pay the bills."

"I'm sorry to hear that. Hope you get them for a while around the holidays."

"She claimed she wanted the holiday, and then, turns out the trainer dude she was seeing didn't want kids at the holidays. But, this year, I had to work, so it was too bad." He smiled. "Sorry, I guess I shouldn't be happy, but he took off for San Diego without her. So, she has the kids for Christmas."

"How many?"

"I have the same thing as you—my boy is ten, and my little girl is five."

"Mine are nine and six."

"Just about the same."

Shayne shifted, pulling his scarf higher around his face; it was really cold in the garage.

"What's the weather doing? Can you see from there?"

"It's still dark and gray, but no snow."

"I'm just saying, I hope your dad can carry through his plan to get us somewhere before Gabe

Lange makes his break. Because, if not, well, it's going to be one hell of a Christmas."

"This is just ridiculous," Morwenna said.

Her father was pacing in the parlor; Stacy was trying to distract Connor and Genevieve with their new toys, but the children had picked up on the tension in the air.

Mike walked to the window. "The snow is deep. If it starts up again and we're walking down to the tavern, someone could really get hurt. I wish it would just do something, one way or the other."

"Well, it's like an ice age out there," Morwenna said. "I'm going to get blankets, and we'll go and spell Bobby and Shayne. They have to be half-frozen, and we've got to do something for both those men, since we've no idea which man is the good one."

"Gabe is really nice," Genevieve said. "How could he be a bad man?"

Mike looked at his granddaughter. He walked over to her, hunkered down and pulled her to him, hugging her tenderly. "Sometimes, it's just hard to tell. And sometimes, we have to really listen and weigh everything that's going on. Sometimes, wolves wear sheep's clothing," he said.

"I'll get the blankets, Dad," Morwenna said.

"There are plenty extra in the hall closet," Stacy said. "And there are some of those little hot packets that you all use when you go out sometimes. They're in a box in the closet, too. Hang on. I'll fix a couple of thermoses with coffee," Stacy said.

"We don't have to baby either of them, Stacy," Mike said.

"Keeping someone alive is hardly babying them!" she said indignantly.

"We're not killing anyone," Mike said wearily.

"I just have a bad time myself not believing Gabe," Stacy said.

Mike stood and looked at his wife. "We're not disbelieving him, Stacy. We're being safe."

He indicated the children. Stacy nodded. "But coffee won't be a bad thing."

"No, Stacy," Mike said. "You fix those thermoses."

Ten minutes later, Morwenna and her father

started out of the house, each holding a thermos, a blanket and a handful of heat packs.

As they neared the garage, Mike warned, "Morwenna, take care. Please. I don't think that guy could possibly find anything in the storage shed to hurt anyone with, but…remember, words can be a dangerous weapon. *Kind* words can be dangerous. That man was a guest in our house…he made us all laugh. But it could have all been a lie. Don't fall for anything, please?"

"I'm not going to fall for a man I don't know. Come on—you know that I'm involved with someone else."

He was silent as they walked for a minute; she could hear the loud crunching sound their feet made in the snow.

"And I know that even while you've cheerfully explained to us why this 'someone else' isn't here, you're trying to sell yourself on the same explanation. Just be careful. I can see that Gabe Lange could be a very attractive man."

"Dad! I was raised by a prosecutor, and I live in Manhattan. I'm nearly as suspicious of all humanity as you." She kissed his cheek, and turned, heading for the shed.

Bobby hadn't closed the door; he was standing in the door frame, hugging himself, and looking as if he was nearly shriveled with cold.

"Go back to the house," she told him. "My turn to take over."

He nodded to her gratefully. "That blanket for me?"

"No, you're heading to the house. It's for Gabe."

"Oh, yeah, makes sense. You going to be okay? You're sure?"

"Fine. Go," she said.

She gave him a little shove and looked into the shed. Gabe was seated on the floor against the wall, and like Bobby, he was curled in on himself as much as was humanly possible.

"Here," she said, tossing down the blanket. He tried to catch it awkwardly with his tied hands. She came close enough to drape it over him, and then carefully stretched out her arm to give him the heat packs. "I have coffee for you, too, but you can put those down your shirt. They'll warm you up for a good hour or so, maybe even two hours."

He nodded, apparently familiar with the little beanbaglike sacks. Morwenna could appreciate her mother's wisdom in seeing that the men were handcuffed with their hands at the front of their bodies rather than behind; she wasn't sure she would have wanted the task of trying to slip the heat packs down into his clothing. It was disconcerting to come even this close.

He managed to get the packs beneath his clothing. Keeping her distance, she handed him the thermos.

"Thanks," he told her. He opened the thermos and took a long swallow of coffee.

"Makes a man feel like he might thaw out again one day," he told her.

"Sure," she said.

"That's better. May be the best coffee I've ever had," he said.

"I'm sure my mother would be glad."

"How's she doing?" he asked.

"My mother? She's fine, of course. We're all

going to be fine. We'll watch both of you until we can get you down to the tavern," Morwenna said.

"Thank God," he murmured.

She stared at him.

"I've been telling you the truth. And when we reach the tavern, you'll know that. Is the weather clearing?"

Morwenna hesitated. It had grown quite dark earlier, but it did seem now that it was beginning to lighten.

"I think so," she said.

"Then we'll be able to leave soon… How about you?" he asked. "How are you holding up?"

"I'm fine."

"And I'm sorry. This is a tough Christmas for you."

"No, it's not."

"Sorry, I just meant—"

"You meant the fact that 'boy toy,' as my brothers call him, didn't bother to come with me," Morwenna said irritably.

"Look, I'm sorry."

"I know, sure. And maybe he's just not the right one for me. And maybe he's enjoying beach bunnies in Cancún."

Gabe grinned. "If he is, he's a fool."

"Your lips to God's ear!" she said.

He laughed. "Something like that. Honestly, I'm just anxious that we move before…well, he's a tricky devil, that one. DeFeo. I'm grateful that your family didn't just believe him. I'm afraid that he'll pull something, and everyone will be in danger."

"I thought he was just a thief."

"You can never trust a cornered thief."

Morwenna stepped away from the door for a moment, studying the sky again. It did seem to be clearing, but not in the ordinary way. It appeared almost as if the light was breaking right above the house, like a giant golden ball, and rays of darkness ebbed into it, and then curled back, ebbing away again.

"We should be able to go soon," she said curtly. She frowned. The front door to the house had opened. Genevieve, cradling her precious teddy bear, was stepping out of the house alone.

"What the heck is she doing?" Morwenna wondered.

Gabe stumbled to his feet, coming to the doorway.

"No!" Morwenna called suddenly.

Genevieve was trying to come out, to see for herself what they were doing. Whatever distraction her mother had been employing with them, it wasn't working.

The little girl was sneaking out—and trying to make sure that she wasn't being seen.

Morwenna could see that her niece meant to approach the shed from the cliff side. Since she was trying not to be seen, she was running around in a wide fashion; she knew that she wasn't allowed to go too far around the house, and yet it suddenly seemed as if she didn't remember. She was a child—a curious child. Morwenna wasn't half as angry as she was afraid.

If she went too far, which she could easily do in

the snow, she'd be on uneven ground, and could tumble down a hundred feet or so.

"No!" Morwenna cried.

Too late.

Genevieve let out a shrill scream as she stepped into the snow…and hit nothing beneath it. As Morwenna bolted across the yard, Genevieve began to fall.

Chapter 7

"We can go out soon," Shayne heard his mother say. She'd been sitting beneath the tree with Genevieve, polishing her nails with a pink color from the package Morwenna had given her, when Shayne had first come in. He thanked God for his mother; she loved his children and she was good with them.

But now, coming back to the parlor from the kitchen, Shayne saw that Stacy was looking out the window. He knew that she was anxious. The kids were growing increasingly restless. Of course, if it was storming, they knew they had to stay in. But they'd been anxious to help with the turkey dinner, and now, Stacy wasn't cooking, and Christmas Day had taken a drastic turn.

"The clouds—or whatever!—are just sitting up there," Stacy said, staring out at the sky. "It's just gray and…actually clearing, maybe."

She turned around suddenly.

"Genevieve?"

Connor was playing with the electronic game he'd gotten. He didn't look up.

"Connor, where did Genevieve go?" Stacy asked.

Connor looked up. "She was right here," he said, frowning.

Stacy looked back to the window and gasped.

"Oh, my God! She's on the side path!" Stacy cried.

Shayne bolted for the door and threw it open, unaware of the blast of frigid air that hit him. Genevieve had disappeared beyond the snow.

"My God!" he cried, and raced to the side path

that was so pretty in summer, so treacherous in winter.

"Genevieve!" His daughter's name tore from his throat.

In an instant, a fraction of a second in time, he realized that he'd been a bitter fool; that even with the pain of the divorce, he'd been the luckiest man in the world. He had two beautiful, healthy children, and they were worth everything in the world.

And now...

As he ran, he could see his sister coming from the opposite direction. And someone was behind her, and then, overtaking her.

Gabe Lange.

Hands still tied, he was moving like cannon shot, a blur in the snow and the gray. Then, he cleanly disappeared.

He had pitched himself down the ledge, toward Genevieve. Morwenna screamed and followed him.

Shayne heard his heart thundering, heard the

gasp of his breath as he reached the path and be-yond; the ledge. And he stopped himself in time.

Gabe had managed to get himself down the slope and wedged next to some kind of brush; he'd prevented Genevieve from tumbling farther with the length of his body. He was struggling to keep his grasp on whatever bush or outcrop of rock was beneath the snow. And Morwenna was just above the two; he could see the branch she held—naked and thin, stripped bare of green, as if it were a skeletal hand reaching for her instead of the other way around.

"Hold still! I'll get rope!" Shayne shouted.

He turned to head back to the house; his mother was behind him, terror in her eyes. She was ready to pitch herself down the mountain, but Shayne grabbed her shoulders.

"Mom! The rope, the cord of nylon rope in the kitchen—go get the whole thing, quickly, please!"

"Oh, Shayne!" she cried.

"Mom, go!"

She turned and fled back to the house; he'd never seen her move so fast.

"Hang on!" he called down the slope.

"Hanging on!" Gabe called up.

Bobby and Connor came running out behind Stacy, who now had the rope. Shayne looked around; there was nothing close enough that was steady and stable to work the rope. Bobby hurried to him, seeing the problem. "You and me, bro. You and me!" he said.

He nodded. "I'm bigger. I'll be the anchor, you the control."

Bobby didn't argue with him; they had perhaps seconds before something down the slope began to give. He expertly knotted the nylon around himself while Bobby made a loop with the other end.

Bobby stood at the precipice, testing his footing. He called down to Gabe. "I've got a loop— coming your way."

Shayne angled himself down on the ground, using his weight as an anchor as Bobby tossed the rope down. It fell almost to Genevieve on the first try, and Bobby cursed beneath his breath. Shayne lowered his head, praying. He heard his sister cry up. "Bobby, I've got it. It's good. I'm getting it to Gabe and Genevieve."

"Got it!" Gabe called.

Shayne heard Genevieve's terrified tears then, and he winced, gritting his teeth, digging in farther. The ground was so slick, with patches of ice beneath the snow. He felt something on his legs; his mother had thrown herself down into the snow, too. They looked at one another, and despite his terror, he offered her a weak smile. "Thanks, Mom. We're going to do this."

She nodded grimly.

"I can't! I can't!" Genevieve cried. "Auntie Wenna, I'm so scared."

"Let Gabe get the rope around you. Your daddy is up there. He's going to get you."

"Bobby?" Shayne asked.

His brother was hunkered down, trying to guide the rope, but Bobby glanced at him. "Gabe is getting the loop around her. Morwenna is talking to her, assuring her."

Shayne was aware of the soft sound of sniffles near him. He looked around. Connor was just standing there, frozen as he watched, too little to help, too big not to know what was going on.

And he was surely blaming himself that his sister had slipped out.

"Okay!" Morwenna called up. "She's secure!"

Bobby started to pull on the rope. Shayne heard Genevieve sniffling and crying again. As Bobby secured the rope, Shayne began to inch backward.

Bobby swore suddenly; Shayne saw Connor make a dive.

"What?" he cried hoarsely.

"It was stuck—Connor slipped it. We're good. Keep moving."

His daughter wasn't even heavy; she was a little thing. And yet he felt as if he strained as he never had before, as if each millisecond was years in the making.

"I've got her!" Bobby cried, and Shayne dared look up again. Bobby was falling back from the ledge, Genevieve in his arms. Shayne lowered his head, trying to stop the shaking that had seized hold of his body.

Thank God, thank God, thank God, thank God…

His instinct was to rise and grab his daughter;

he knew he couldn't do so. He called out to his mother. "Mom, get Gen. Get her inside, please. Connor, get Gramps. Get him out of the garage—now, please, Connor."

He heard the footsteps in the snow. Morwenna wasn't heavy—maybe a hundred and twenty pounds. But the snow was slick, and the hauling was hard. "Bobby?"

"I've got it back down. Morwenna has the rope...it's around her. Now, Shayne, now, I'm hauling it up."

Again, Shayne began his backward crawl in the snow. He kept fit; being a physician had made him do so, but he felt every muscle, and it seemed every speck of blood and bone in him, ache with the effort.

As he thought he might not make it, his father came running across the snow; he reached Bobby's side and took on some of the weight, and Shayne inched backward again.

He heard his sister cry out. "I'm here—I've caught the ledge. Just...your hand, Dad."

Shayne looked up again. Mike MacDougal had

Morwenna in his arms. The two of them fell backward in the snow, Morwenna half laughing and half crying in their father's arms.

"We've still got Gabe down there!" Bobby reminded them all.

"If you were smart, you'd leave him there."

Shayne twisted to see who was talking. Of course, Mike had left his post at the garage door; Luke DeFeo had followed him out.

"If you're really law enforcement," Mike said, "you'll remember that you catch the criminals, and the justice system sees to punishment."

"And if you're an ADA," DeFeo countered, "you know that half the scum of the earth winds up in court—and then walking."

"Shayne, you ready?" Bobby asked. "Rope is going down again. Can you handle it?"

"Yes," Shayne said.

And yes, he would.

"Go! You've got Dad to help you lever the weight."

This time, it was going to be really hard; Gabe

Lange was at least six-two, and had to weigh a well-muscled two hundred–plus pounds.

"Damn!" Bobby swore. He'd not gotten the rope down far enough.

As he pulled it up to toss it down again, they all heard the cracking of a branch, as loud as thunder in the crisp and silent air of the tension-filled winter morning.

"Hurry!" Morwenna breathed.

"Got it, got it," Bobby assured her.

He tossed the rope again.

They heard Gabe shouting from below. "I have it!"

Just as the echo of his words died, they heard a crack like a gunshot; it was the end of the bush that had broken Gabe's fall down the slope.

Shayne felt himself jerked forward as Gabe's weight fell fully on the rope.

Morwenna screamed, throwing herself on Shayne to further anchor him; Mike lunged forward, catching the rope with Bobby, and they both leaned back, trying to brace their boots against the slick white snow.

"Wenna, back…inch back little by little," Shayne said.

She obeyed him; she wasn't much on size, but the fact that she was there with him, clinging to him as if he were salvation itself, gave him strength. She braced his legs, moving as slowly as a snail, adding weight to his anchor as he painfully wormed his way back, feeling as if his shoulders would break and his spine would snap if they didn't make it soon.

But then, just when he thought he wouldn't make it, the pressure eased up. He and Morwenna had been trying so hard to keep moving that they actually slid backward a foot when the tension on the rope eased.

Again, he dared to look up. Mike had dragged Gabe up the last few feet. And now he, Bobby and Gabe were lying halfway entangled with one another by the slope, gasping for breath, laughing with relief and congratulating one another.

Shayne rolled to his back and looked up at the sky.

It had cleared; the dark clouds were gone.

He glanced to the side. Still handcuffed, Luke DeFeo was looking on.

"He's a damn good actor," he said quietly to Shayne.

"I don't give a damn if it was an act or not," Shayne said. "My daughter and my sister are alive."

Morwenna, showered, changed and headed downstairs. She could hear her father speaking to her brother Bobby, and she stopped before reaching the parlor.

"He showered, got into dry warm clothes and let me put the ropes right back on him," Bobby said. "Dad, I just can't see how the man could be any kind of killer."

"I have to admit, Bobby, I just don't see it either. But the thing is, we still don't *know*. What if DeFeo is right?"

"Dad, Gabe pitched himself over a cliff to save Genevieve," Bobby said.

"So did your sister," Mike said huskily.

"Morwenna is my hero, Dad. But she's Genevieve's aunt. Gabe was ready to give his life for a little girl he just met."

She heard her father sigh deeply. "I know that, Bobby. But the sky has cleared. We're getting these guys down to the tavern. Someone there will have some way to communicate with the rest of the world. And if we're right, and Gabe is a good guy, we'll know it then."

Morwenna hurried down the stairs.

"Where are our—prisoners now?" she asked.

"In the kitchen," her father told her.

"With Shayne?"

"Shayne is trying to make Genevieve and Connor understand that they still have to learn to listen to what they're told," Bobby said.

"Then who is watching the prisoners?" she asked.

"Your mother," Mike said.

"Mom?"

Mike grinned. "Don't underestimate the power of a mother and grandmother, Morwenna," he told her. "She's grateful to Gabe, but she's hard as nails when she wants to be. She knows we're all going to start down to the tavern."

Morwenna stared at her father and Bobby with surprise, and then hurried into the kitchen.

Both men were seated on stools by the island workstation with steaming cups in front of them. It wasn't coffee; Morwenna smelled the aroma of chicken soup.

Stacy was seated away from them at the far end, the shotgun in her hand.

She glanced at Morwenna as she entered. "Make sure you're dressed good and warm," she told her daughter. "We're going to leave as soon as everyone is ready."

"We're walking down, I take it?" she asked her mother, eyeing the two men. They were at opposite sides of the table, but Stacy had seen to it that neither could possibly reach out and grab her—or the shotgun.

"We have to. There isn't a plausible path a car could make anywhere on the mountain right now," her mother said. "Yesterday was dangerous, and there's been more snow since then. Last night, late in the night, I woke up, and I saw that it was snowing again."

Morwenna couldn't help but look across the table at Gabe. He looked at her with a grin and a shrug.

"On this walk, you'd better keep a close eye on Gabe Lange," DeFeo warned. "Don't you people see? He figured that once he'd saved the little girl, you'd be so grateful, you'd untie him."

"He could have died," Morwenna pointed out.

"Yes, but he's facing life in prison or a death sentence if you get him down the mountain," DeFeo said. "The Commonwealth of Virginia still carries out the death penalty when the judge determines that it's appropriate. And you people still don't know the half of what he's capable of."

"We've established that," Morwenna said.

"Fine—take your chances walking down to the tavern," DeFeo said.

"That's what we're doing," Stacy said firmly.

"Stacy!"

Mike's voice sounded from the parlor.

"Yes, Mike?"

"We're ready. Head them on out," he called.

"You heard my husband," Stacy said. "Rise slowly and carefully, gentlemen, one at a time, please, and keep your distance from each other as we head out."

The men rose. Gabe stared at Luke. "After you."

"No, no. I wouldn't be so rude. After you," DeFeo said.

"DeFeo, you first!" Morwenna said. "And I'll be behind you with a frying pan, and trust me, I actually know how to use one on someone's head!"

"Careful not to get in my line of fire," Stacy said lightly.

DeFeo started out. For a moment, Morwenna thought he was going to make a lunge for the knives in the wooden holder on the counter; she quickly made good on her threat and reached for the copper-bottomed frying pan above her head, but it appeared he had just stumbled; he righted himself, balancing against the counter as he headed out.

In the parlor, Stacy handed the shotgun over to Mike. Shayne had brought the children down, dressed in dry snowsuits for the walk down to the tavern. Genevieve was clinging to Connor; Connor had an arm around his sister. She was still white-faced and silent.

Morwenna knew that Shayne had to have done something to discipline her, no matter how grateful he was that she was alive. What she had done was against what she'd been told, and she had certainly been terrified by her misdeed.

Still, she offered her niece a smile. Genevieve looked up at her brother, and then ran to Morwenna, burying her face against Morwenna's thigh.

"Sweetie, we're all right," Morwenna said gently. She lifted the little girl, and looked at Shayne. She didn't think that her brother had been too hard on his daughter.

"Head on out," Mike said grimly.

Bobby led the way; Morwenna followed, Genevieve in her arms, Connor close behind. Ahead of the others a little, Morwenna asked Genevieve, "What made you run out like that? Daddy told you never to go near the path in winter."

Genevieve didn't answer. She laid her head against Morwenna's neck.

"Sweetie?"

"I had to make sure you didn't hurt him."

"Hurt—Gabe?"

Genevieve nodded.

"What made you think someone was hurting him?" Morwenna asked.

Genevieve looked up at her without speaking.

"She decided to look at the angel, and she dropped it, and she was all freaked out for some reason," Connor said, shaking his head with the wisdom of his older-brother years.

"Honey, the angel on the tree is just an ornament," Morwenna said. "And no ornament in the world is worth risking one pretty little hair on your head."

"It didn't break," Genevieve whispered.

"Well, that's good. But it doesn't matter."

"It did matter. I almost broke it," Genevieve said. "We should never hurt our angels. Angels are there to protect us."

"She's just not going to make any sense," Connor said sagely.

"I understand," Morwenna said, smiling. "But the ornament didn't break, and it is an ornament, Genevieve, a pretty ornament that makes us think of angels. But it's all really all right."

"Follow me—I know the road best," Bobby said. He looked back at her and grinned. "I am the baby, you know. Adult baby now, of course, but I've spent the most time with the folks around here lately. I'll keep you from sinking into the snow." He frowned, arching a brow to Morwenna. "How long do you think you can carry her?"

Morwenna wondered that herself. The snow was deep, at least two feet, and every step they took was something of an effort.

"I think the snow may be taller than she is," Morwenna said.

"We can trade off," Bobby assured her.

Morwenna turned back. Shayne had positioned himself between DeFeo and Morwenna and his children; Gabe followed DeFeo, and her mother walked by her father's side at the rear.

She shifted Genevieve's weight. It was true; Genevieve might be a little bit of a girl, but she got heavy quickly as they floundered in the snow. The path, even with Bobby leading, was rough; there were patches of ice, and he warned her about them as he slipped and slid his way in the lead. They were going downward, and though, beneath the snow, the road was decent, it was bound to be difficult going.

Her arms began to ache, but she was determined to make it another ten minutes; Bobby was the lead, testing the ground. She was afraid that Shayne would wind up with muscle spasms, after all that he'd been through, dragging everyone back up the slope. Her father had the shotgun, and she was afraid that her mother would snap somewhere along the line. Stacy could be so strong—but how strong?

"We are idiots, you know," Bobby said.

She looked at him, smiling. "I'm certain we often are—on many levels. But why are you saying that?"

"We have little sleds! Why didn't we bring one of the sleds—we could have pulled the children."

"Because we weren't thinking. Because we don't know who is a convict and who is a good guy."

"All right...but we should have thought of the sled," Bobby said.

Morwenna hugged Genevieve more tightly.

She winced, thinking of the horrible minutes she'd been caught on the ledge. First, trying to get Genevieve up. She'd never imagined what it could be like to be so terrified for her own life, and even more afraid for the life of the little girl. Terrified, and frozen.

Gabe can't be bad! she told herself. *She could recall his words; she could almost hear his voice aloud as she remembered the way he had assured her: "It's all right. I've got a hold here that's solid enough for a few minutes. I've got Genevieve. Just get the rope...there, you can do it. Have faith in yourself, Morwenna, you can do it."*

And still, when DeFeo spoke, warning them that people could appear to be so many things that they weren't, doubt crept in.

He could have let Genevieve go; he could have even reached for her, and killed her on the ledge.

Ah, but then what would he have done? As DeFeo said, he was securely "handcuffed" by the rope. He would have died himself on the ledge, with no one to haul him back up.

He'd never *had* to go over the ledge; he'd risked his life to do it.

But if there was the possibility he was facing a death sentence...

Doubt!

Why was doubt so much easier than faith? Or, could doubt and care be associated with simple intelligence. And where the hell did instinct fit into it all? Her instinct was to trust Gabe, but could it be that people were too easily led?

"The cemetery is ahead on the left!" she heard her mother call out to Bobby.

"The cemetery?" she asked incredulously.

Bobby turned to her.

"Mom still intends to say her Christmas prayers at the family grave site and tomb, come heaven or hell!" Bobby told her.

"There's too much snow! We won't even see the graves," Morwenna protested.

"You try to tell her that!"

The old stone wall of the little cemetery in the mountains was, at least, still above the snow. They reached it in about a minute, and Morwenna realized that Bobby had kept them on a straight-and-narrow path, following the line of the road. There was a curve in the wall ahead—the entry, which could be accessed by cars when cars could get on the road.

With any luck, she thought, *the gate would be locked!*

But the gate wasn't locked.

Bobby looked at her. "Not our lucky day," he said lightly.

Despite the fact that the gray clouds that had hovered earlier had moved on, the cemetery seemed shadowed and eerie. It lay beneath the naked and fragmented branches of trees, with only an evergreen here and there to remind the living that spring would come again.

The snow lay heavy over many of the graves,

and they were clearly the first ones to brave the road into the graveyard that day. The tips of a few stones just peeked over the snow in some areas.

Bobby was careful to keep them on the roadway through the graveyard—that way, at least, no one would trip over any of the stones, markers or memorials that lay beneath the blanket of white.

"Just ahead," Connor murmured.

Morwenna was glad; she was going to have to trade off with someone. The world was icy cold; she could see her breath coming from her in a fog, but her arm burned like a fiery rod, the muscles giving in after the long walk.

She paused for a minute, staring ahead. Her mother's maiden name was Byrne; the name, she had been told, meant raven, and a large raven stood guard on the wrought-iron fence that led to the little vault and the graves that surrounded it.

High atop the vault, there was a beautiful marble angel. The angel wasn't lowered upon one knee in sorrow, but rather seemed to stand tall against the wind, robes and wings flying behind it as it proudly faced the world. She'd always liked the angel. She wished, in fact, that she'd at least draw something so beautiful at some time in her life.

Bobby pushed hard at the wrought-iron gate; it creaked and squealed, fighting against the snow as it scraped open. Morwenna entered the enclosed area, and set Genevieve up on one of the steps to the vault that was still higher than the snow.

She heard the others pile in behind her, and she thought of the incongruity of their group there; the kids, her mom, determined to say her Christmas prayers at the family grave site, and her father, ready to pray with her mother while still keeping a sharp eye on their prisoners, his shotgun at the ready.

"Mom?" Morwenna said.

Stacy moved forward to the steps, hugging Genevieve to her side, and looking out at them. "Christmas Day, again, and we're all together, and I'm so grateful. I want to thank God for the family that came before me. I want to tell my folks that I loved them very much. And I want, most of all, to say thank-you for the family that I have now. Guide us, be with us. Keep us safe."

"You're definitely not safe yet," DeFeo said quietly.

"Will you stop—this is a sacred time for my mother!" Shayne snapped angrily.

As he spoke, they were startled as a large black bird suddenly shot through the trees, letting out an eerie shriek. Morwenna ducked as it flew by them.

Stacy watched the bird without flinching. "It's a raven!" she said, and laughed. "Mike, I think that the family is grateful that we're here."

"All right, all right, it's a great and wonderful family day," Luke DeFeo said. "Let me help. Bow your heads in prayer!"

Startled, Morwenna watched him, but slowly, one by one, the other members of her family did so.

"Praise be to the God and Father of our Lord Jesus Christ," DeFeo said, his voice ringing clearly, "who has blessed us in the heavenly realms with every spiritual blessing in Christ. For he chose us in him before the creation of the world to be holy and blameless in his sight. In love he predestined us to be adopted as his sons through Jesus Christ, in accordance with his pleasure and will to the praise of his glorious grace, which he has freely given us in the One he loves. In him we have redemption through his blood, the forgiveness of sins, in accordance with the riches of God's grace that he lavished on us with all wisdom and understanding. And he made known to us the mystery of his will according to his good pleasure, which he purposed in Christ, to be put into effect when the times will have reached their fulfillment to bring all things in heaven and on earth together under one head, even Christ."

He finished speaking.

"Very nice," Gabe said. "Ephesians, I:3–10."

DeFeo arched a brow to him, a look of satisfaction on his face.

Stacy didn't notice either of them. "Amen!" she said happily.

Morwenna found that she was studying the two men; Gabe didn't seem disturbed, but he was watching DeFeo curiously. DeFeo looked very proud of himself, as if he had proven a point.

"Thank you, Father," Gabe said then, smiling as he looked up at the angel. "Thank you for this family, for the pride and courage and love to be found among them, even here, among those who have passed over to your realm. May you bless the lives of those who have proven to be so kind, and who value human life, even among those they know not as friends or enemies."

"Amen," Stacy said again, and this time, her family followed suit. "Anyone else?" she asked.

"Dear God and Jesus," Genevieve said. "Happy birthday again. Also, could you please make it just a little bit warmer?"

"Amen!" Bobby said, laughing. And he added, "This was lovely, Mom. But maybe we should move on."

Morwenna heard a slight rumbling. She looked up. It seemed that the clouds were coming back again. And again, strangely, light remained among them. The angel on the tomb stood proud in a fierce ray of light, the sun, somehow, shooting down upon it through all the turbulence in the atmosphere.

Shayne came to her side. "I'll take Gen," he said quietly. "I can't believe you made it this far."

She smiled at him, and touched his cheek. She found herself thinking of the way they had fought like cats and dogs as children, and she was suddenly aware that he would have killed himself, not just to get his daughter back, but her, too.

"She's not so heavy. Okay, I'm lying. My arms are killing me. But you must still be feeling some muscle pain of your own, huh?"

"Yeah, but it's all over," he said, grinning. "My arms can take a little more."

He bent down to pick up his daughter.

"It's cold, Daddy," Genevieve said.

"Actually, sweetheart," Stacy said, "I think you prayed it a tiny bit warmer."

"We're almost down to the tavern, baby," Shayne said. "We'll get some nice hot cocoa there—hey, and I'll bet they have turkey on the menu, too."

"It won't be as good as Gram's turkey," Genevieve said.

"No, it won't be, but it will be warm."

"Move 'em out!" Bobby said, taking the lead again.

Morwenna paused, looking up at the angel that rode so beautifully over the tomb.

She smiled suddenly. She barely remembered her mother's parents now, but they had been good people. Hardy mountain stock, very independent—and very loving at the same time. They hadn't built the tomb, of course. The tomb dated back to the early eighteen hundreds.

And yet, someone, way back in her family, had known what a tomb should offer; not sorrow and pain, but pride and hope.

"Morwenna!"

She started; her father was waiting for her, and nervously watching the procession that had gone ahead of him at the same time.

"Coming, Dad!" she said.

But as he started away, she said her own prayer.

"Thanks," she murmured huskily, adding quickly, "Thank you for Genevieve, and thank you for me, and for us all...and help us! Please help us do what's right."

She almost expected the angel to move.

It didn't.

She turned and hurried out after her family. It was still another twenty to thirty minutes down the slippery road until they reached the little tavern nestled in the mountains among the pines.

Chapter 8

Breaking onto the last stretch, Bobby was glad to see that the lights were on at Scott's Tavern, or, as a neon subtitle below the main sign stated, Scott's Ye Olde Tavern and Grill.

There were even two cars parked in the lot, but Bobby didn't think they'd be going anywhere soon; there would have to be some major digging done before the roads were navigable. He wondered if people from the tavern had held off on the digging because, like his family, they'd expected snow to begin falling in earnest again at any point.

He turned back. Now, DeFeo was heading along behind him, Gabe behind Defeo, and behind Gabe, Shayne was walking with Connor's hand in his. His father had Genevieve and walked alongside his mother, and following behind, ever aware she was carrying a loaded shotgun, came Morwenna.

"Yes, we've made it," Gabe said, coming up so that he stood next to Luke DeFeo, and giving him a smile.

"Not really, not yet," DeFeo said.

Then Bobby wasn't really sure what happened. He didn't know if DeFeo went after Gabe, or if Gabe went after DeFeo, or even if one of them had slipped on a patch of black ice, which knocked them over the embankment together.

Either way, they were sliding away fast.

"Hey!" he shouted to the others.

Shayne, of course, had seen what had happened and was already racing up to Bobby; Bobby started down through the snow and brush for the men.

They were still rolling, snapping branches and twigs off dead brush as they sped along. He began to run, leaping over obstacles, aware that Shayne was right behind him.

"Hey, stop!" he yelled at the two men.

They were fighting in desperate, awkward moves, since they both had their hands cuffed or tied. DeFeo got his arms around Gabe's neck, and Bobby shouted again, seeing the man's face begin to turn red. But Gabe was surprisingly agile and strong, throwing himself forward so that DeFeo was thrown over his head and sent into the brush again. When DeFeo would have risen and charged, he was stopped by the loud sound of a bullet blasting into the air.

"Stop it! Now!" Morwenna, as fierce as a lioness, was standing up on the embankment, the shotgun in her hand. But even as she spoke, Gabe was at DeFeo's side; he wasn't attacking him. He was giving him a hand to get to his feet.

As he neared the two of them, he heard them talking.

"Great! Give me a hand, huh? Oh, how *saintly* of you," DeFeo said.

"You've got on borrowed togs," Gabe said. "You want to be careful with them."

That sounded odd. Maybe he'd heard him wrong. Maybe he was just speaking lightly. But why get into a fight with a guy that might have killed one of them and worry about *togs*. *Clothing?*

"Come on, you two," Bobby said, determined to sound as fierce as his sister looked, standing on the embankment. "Let's go. The tavern is just ahead."

To his amazement, they both listened to him. Gabe led the way. Luke DeFeo followed.

"Still need the cops," DeFeo murmured.

Gabe ignored him. Bobby waited, following as the two men headed back up to the road.

"What the hell was that?" Morwenna demanded when everyone reached the road.

"Hey, we fell," DeFeo said. He looked at Gabe. "But you, you…"

"That's the tavern, right in front of us?" he said.

Morwenna looked at him. "That's the tavern."

"They still have electricity. Maybe they'll have internet service, or working phones," Gabe said.

"Maybe they will, and maybe they won't," DeFeo said. "You haven't won anything yet, you know."

"Ah," Gabe said, "but my glass is always half-full."

Morwenna could have kissed the ground when they finally walked into the tavern. Whether she was right or not, she didn't know—but the responsibility for deciding which man was telling the truth had, at the least, been expanded. Once they walked through the door, she saw her parents' old friend, Mac Scott, behind the bar.

As long as she could remember, Mac had been behind the bar. He owned Scott's, which was a small legend, in a way. To anyone who lived in the area, or visited the remote mountain area with any frequency, Mac Scott's place was *the* place.

It was the *only* place.

Nestled in a little valley in the heights, it lay on the outskirts of what might optimistically be called a village. It was next to a shop that sold cold-weather gear and hiking and climbing equipment, and down and across the single street from the church, and across from the gas station—slash—convenience store that accommodated the area. A rangers' station was down another level, and the little area served all those who kept homes, part-time or year-round, in the mid area of the Virginia Blue Ridge peaks.

"Morwenna! Morwenna MacDougal!" Mac called from behind the bar. He was a big, tall man, a mountain man whose ancestors had been in the region for years.

He still looked like a massive highlander.

"Mac, hey," she said.

"Is the family with you?" Mac asked.

"Right behind me."

"You're early. What, did Stacy cook turkey for breakfast?" Mac asked.

Stacy shook her head, hurrying over to the bar as the others filed in behind her. "Mac, we have a problem. Do you have a working phone, or internet—or any way to contact anyone? We had a stranger hurt out by us—"

"Wow. Was Shayne there then? Thank God that boy is a doctor," Mac said. He frowned, and she realized that he was looking over her shoulder and seeing Gabe and Luke DeFeo being ushered in—the one with his hands tied, and the other in cuffs.

He looked back at Stacy, arching a black shaggy brow. "Shayne's got some bedside manner," he said quietly.

"Very funny. The first guy, Gabe, the lighter-haired one, said that he was a cop, and he'd gone down in a skirmish with a con. The second guy came and said that *he* was the cop, and the first guy was the con, and we have no way of knowing who is telling the truth," Morwenna explained. "Neither has ID."

"Well, hell," Mac said.

"You—that booth," her father told Gabe. "And you, DeFeo—you in that booth over there."

Mac looked at Morwenna again. "You've got to be kidding me."

"Mac, does it look like I'm joking?" Morwenna asked.

Genevieve ran over to join her at the bar, crawling up on a stood to smile at Mac and reach out for him. In Genevieve's six-year-old world, she realized, nothing precluded a hug from an old friend.

Mac reached over the bar, and Genevieve hugged him. Mac was her "big bear," she always said.

"Hey, there, little missy," Mac said. "Merry Christmas."

Frowning, he looked at Morwenna.

"So, can you help?" she asked.

"Morwenna, I'm sorry—my cable has been out forever. I've still got electricity, and I was counting my blessings for that! But I can't get anything on television except for the local channels. And I haven't been able to call out on the bar phone or on my cell since yesterday morning. Once that snow started coming in yesterday, everything went wacko."

Morwenna frowned, looking toward the back booth. "Who else is here?" She craned her neck, trying to see who might be sitting in the high-backed booths.

"The Williamsons and their two boys—do you know them? Brian Williamson's folks owned his house, just like your mom's folks owned your house on up the mountain," Mac said. He was talking to Morwenna again, but looking over at the booths—and Mike MacDougal, with his shot-gun.

"Have they been stuck here?" Morwenna asked. "Snowbound, I mean?"

"No," Mac said. "They walked up, the same way you all came down."

As they spoke, of course, the Williamson family noted that there were newcomers at the tavern; Brian Williamson, plumber by day, banjo player upon occasion, rose and walked across the tavern to the booths, frowning as he saw Mike Mac-Dougal with a shotgun.

"Mike, Merry Christmas, and what the hell?" he demanded.

Morwenna watched as her father went through the explanation. "You don't happen to have a working phone on you, do you?" Mike asked Brian.

"No, Mary and I were just talking about that—phones and internet, kaput! The boys were playing pool until a few minutes ago." He looked from one stranger to the next as he spoke. He added firmly, "But you've done well to bring them down here. Now you've got Mac and me and the boys—they're fifteen and seventeen—to make sure that neither of these fellows causes any mischief."

"I'm an officer," Luke said, "an officer of the law, and if anyone in this place had any sense, you'd all realize it. If you help these people keep me incarcerated and that con gets away, I promise you that you'll have hell to pay as well!"

Gabe lowered his head, shaking it, and then looked up at Brian Williamson, and across the pool table and the bar at Mac. "He's a liar. And the MacDougal family knows that I'm not out to hurt any of them."

Mac leaned across the bar. "Who the hell knows which one of you is a liar? Mike, what can I get you to drink? Don't you worry none. You have help around you now to keep an eye on those men."

Morwenna frowned, realizing that the TV was running.

"Mac—you have television. So...how?"

"Yeah, the cable is down, but I jimmied the old antenna. We're getting some local stuff," Mac said. "It comes and goes. Some static, some show. Well, now, you had a long walk down here in the cold. What can I get everyone?"

"Hot chocolate!" Genevieve said, not in the least shy about asking her "big bear" for anything.

"Yeah, sure, thanks," Connor said.

"I'd love a beer," Mike said, still watching both men as he approached the bar.

"Yeah," Shayne said huskily.

"Not me. I'll have a nice Irish coffee," Stacy said, approaching the bar as well.

"Mac, do you have any turkey? My tummy is rumbling," Genevieve said.

"Mac, you're getting a lot of orders here. If I may, I'll come on back and help," Morwenna told him.

He was well equipped for the clientele he got

during the winter season; he had a steamer that made hot chocolate, and it was easy to use. Morwenna figured all the kids were going to want hot chocolate, so she went ahead and made cups for the Williamson boys, too. When she set them on the counter, Bobby was there to take them out for her. Mac was pouring draft beers, and her father was seated on a bar stool then, watching the two men in the booths. Stacy sat by her husband, pulling her granddaughter onto her lap.

"Think Mac does have turkey?" she asked hopefully.

"Mac, got turkey?" Morwenna asked.

"Yes, I got turkey," Mac said. "And I'll just get you situated with drinks, and go on back and get you some food, too," he assured her.

"What about them?" Morwenna asked, looking at her father and indicating the men in the booths. Brian Williamson and his wife, Mary, were watching the two strangers.

"I could go for a beer," Gabe said.

"Give them both a beer. What the hell. Looks like we're all in a fix here," Mike said.

Morwenna poured the drafts for their prisoners, and then walked around to the tables. She set one down in front of Luke DeFeo first, and then one in front of Gabe. As she did so, DeFeo said, "Look! The picture's back on the television. Turn it up, please, someone. Maybe the news will come on and show that Gabe Lange is a wanted man."

He was right; the TV set suddenly went from static to a picture.

They had just missed a news report, but the picture was suddenly clear, and an attractive young anchorwoman was seated at a desk with a similarly attractive young man.

"Happy holidays to our viewers across the world," the woman said.

Morwenna found herself slipping in to sit at the booth across from Gabe, staring up at the screen.

She was startled when Gabe's hand fell on hers. "Remember what I told you before," he said quietly.

"What? Told me about what?"

"About *you*," he said. "You should never just settle. You should never spend your life living out someone else's love, career or goals. The best is out there—the best of everything that will really make you happy. And you will find the way, and the right people in the world. Don't become a hamster on a wheel."

She shook her head, irritated. There was actually something on the television, and she wanted to see the familiar sight of people far away moving across a big flat-screen television. It was sad to realize, but TV was a *norm* in the average life, even when one wasn't exactly watching it.

And maybe the powers that be would break in with a news bulletin!

"People of all faiths and creeds now partake in our American holiday season, which, to everyone, becomes a time of spending their days in either family bonding—"

"Or not!" the man at her side interrupted jokingly.

His co-anchor laughed as she looked at him.

"Yes, and some take off for exotic locations," the woman said. "With that in mind, we've had our reporters around the globe bring us a short video on Christmas—around the globe!" she said.

The screen flashed to a scene at the Vatican where throngs, in their Christmas best, stood in Saint Peter's Square as the pope spoke. The anchorman narrated over the visual clips.

"Isn't it beautiful at the Vatican? For some, it's the holiest of holy days! The scene is familiar at Westminster Abbey in London." The scene switched to England; there was snow on the ground outside the abbey, and it looked like a postcard. Christmas lights fell upon gargoyles and angels, and Morwenna could almost hear Big Ben chiming in the background.

"In areas of the South, we have a different kind of music going on," the young anchorwoman said, and the television screen portrayed a church with far more simple decor; plain pews and a minister directing a choir; for a moment, the music was beautiful and a chorus sang gospel renditions of very old carols.

"Now, it's fun time, too," the anchorwoman said, and they switched to a scene of a couple at a ski resort, the man laughing as the woman nearly fell, uneasy on her skis; she grabbed on to him, and they exchanged a long kiss.

"And, if cold isn't your thing, there are the beaches of Mexico!"

Morwenna looked over at Gabe. His head was down, as if he knew what she was going to see before she saw it.

He seemed to be concentrating.

She frowned, and glanced back at the television.

For a moment, static broke up the picture.

Then the screen straightened.

What was the size and population of Mexico? Morwenna wondered. *The country was certainly fairly large, and the population was well over a hundred million. There must have been hundreds of thousands of tourists besides, and yet...*

There he was on the screen. Alex. Tall, handsome, perfect corporate-America Alex, tanned and well-muscled, looking like a cover model. He was running down the beach in bathing trunks, chasing after...

Yes. Yes, it was Double-D Debbie Richards from Accounting.

And the camera stayed focused on the pair as the sparkling water of the Gulf of Mexico flew up around them in a crystal spray, as Alex caught up with a laughing Debbie, encircled her waist with his arms and crashed with her into the surf.

The screen changed as the newscasters brought their audience to Australia, and then onward to Jerusalem.

Morwenna didn't really see any more of the pictures dancing before her eyes.

She felt Gabe's hand on hers again. She met his eyes.

"You're not surprised," he told her quietly. "And more than that, you're not brokenhearted. You've known that you've been playing a role, and it came to you fairly easily. Morwenna, don't let what you saw eat at you. You're due to have much more in life. Much more that is *real*."

She heard his words; they were nice words. She still felt frozen, as she hadn't once in all the fierce cold that had surrounded them in winter's white chill.

She was barely aware of Gabe's hand on hers.

No matter what he said, it hurt. Seeing Alex up there... She had just said goodbye to him yesterday morning.

Bobby slid into the booth next to her. She was suddenly aware of the world around her again. She could see her mother, still entertaining Genevieve at the bar. Her father was sitting at the bar having a conversation with Brian and Mary Williamson while keeping an eagle eye on the two booths. Shayne had walked back to where Sam and Adam Williamson were playing an electronic game with Connor.

"What's the matter?" he asked her.

"What?" she asked, looking at him.

"You've turned white." He stared at Gabe, his eyes narrowing, as if he suspected that Gabe had said something that had disturbed his sister.

Yes, that's exactly what he thought.

"What did you do?" he demanded of Gabe.

Somehow, those fierce, protective words from

her cheerful, guitar-playing baby brother brought a flush of warmth into her system again.

"He didn't do or say anything," Morwenna said.

"Then...are you sick? Are you all right?" He set the back of his hand on her forehead.

"I'm fine," she assured him.

He glanced at the television.

"Oh!" he said softly. "You're wishing you were in Mexico." He squeezed her arm. "I'm sorry, sis. I guess it's hard to think that you could be lying out on the beach, or splashing in the water—instead of trying to figure out if we have a cop and thief or a cop and a homicidal murderer on our hands."

"I wasn't after a murderer," Gabe said quietly.

"And I wasn't wishing that I was anywhere else," Morwenna said. She looked at her brother, and a smile came to her lips. "Really," she said, and she realized it was the truth. In their day-to-day lives, her brothers were so far away. And they were busy. And it was easy to forget that while she worried about her brothers and their lives, she forgot sometimes just what they meant to her.

And what she meant to them.

"It's okay. *I'm* okay, really. It was just the TV."

Bobby's eyes widened suddenly as he stared at her.

"Oh!" he said.

"What?"

"Mexico, oh, my God! We haven't had a television, and we have it for two minutes...was that *Alex* on the screen? With that girl?"

Double-D Debbie from Accounting.

She didn't say it out loud.

"Oh, Wenna, I'm so sorry," Bobby said.

"It's okay, really. It's okay," she said.

He looked at Gabe. "You *knew*. How the hell did you know?"

Before Gabe could answer, they were all startled by a different voice coming through the speakers. "We are interrupting your local programming for a news bulletin. Be on the lookout for—"

The screen suddenly turned back to snow; no words issued through the speakers, only a fizzing sound that went with the snow.

"Lost it again!" Mac said, walking back from

the kitchen area into the bar. "It's been like that all day, on one minute, and gone the next. Little Miss MacDougal, I will have your turkey out in just a matter of minutes."

"Turkey," Mike echoed, staring at the snow-covered television screen, and then lowering his head as he shook it.

"Can you believe the TV went out right when it did?" Bobby asked rhetorically.

"Yes, I can," Gabe said. His eyes were downcast. He was talking to himself, really, Morwenna thought, and he sounded a little bitter, and somewhat resigned.

"Bobby, dear baby brother, let me out," Morwenna said. "I'm going to go and help Mac with the dinner plates. He's all alone here, and nine of us just plopped into his bar. He definitely needs a hand."

"Sure. I can help, too," Bobby said.

"No, no—two can handle it. You stay here—and keep an eye on him," she said, looking at Gabe.

His eyes met hers. Still that clear green, and so seemingly without guile.

He didn't smile; he didn't say a word. He just looked at her, and when she turned to walk away, she knew that his eyes were following her.

He may not be the con, she thought. But there was something odd going on. It was as if he knew far more about them and their situations than they did.

She turned and stared at Luke DeFeo. He was looking back at her. "We'd love turkey, too, you know. Please," he said politely.

She nodded. "We don't intend to starve anyone."

He smiled.

And it was strange; she thought that he, too, knew something that she didn't.

A chilling thought struck her: What if they were both cons, just playing a game with the family? And what if...?

What if they were both just depending on the decency of the family, waiting for a chance to rob them all blind or—or worse?

She squared her shoulders. There was nothing she could do that they weren't already doing.

Waiting.

Hoping.

Praying.

Shayne finally left his position at the bar and walked over to the booths; Bobby was across from Gabe, keeping an eye on him.

He slid in across from Luke DeFeo.

"You would have seen it. You would have seen that he was the homicidal escaped con if the television hadn't gone out."

"Maybe," Shayne said, reminding himself to maintain a poker face, no matter what the man had to say to him. "And maybe we would have seen that you're a lying scumbag."

DeFeo took a swallow of his beer. His handcuffs clinked together as he did so.

Despite the hindrance, he seemed to really enjoy the beer.

He lifted his glass. "I'm grateful...grateful to your family. At least, you're not treating us like animals. At least, not too much so."

"You're not animals. And, frankly, around my

family, animals are treated like people. My mother is a sucker for any lost puppy or kitten that comes her way."

"And what about you—and yours?" DeFeo asked.

"What do you mean?"

"Oh, yeah, I forgot—you're divorced. I guess it would be the wife who wanted to take in every stray."

Shayne blinked, not speaking for a minute. Yes, of course, over the years, they'd had many a visitor. When a dog or cat made it into their yard without a tag, they kept it, and Cindy spent endless hours walking the streets, putting up flyers and heading to every animal shelter in the area to see that a flyer went up. She raged against those who didn't neuter or spay their pets; she cried over the fate of ill-treated creatures. And, to her credit, any time Cindy hadn't found the rightful owner, she had found someone in need of a stray.

"Sorry, didn't mean to cause you any pain. I know what it can be like. I've gone the route," DeFeo said.

"We're all doing all right," Shayne said.

"Sure, sure, of course."

"Turkey!"

Shayne heard the excited cry come from the bar; it was Genevieve, of course. Mac had decided to bring the first plates out to Shayne's mom and daughter.

But Genevieve squirmed off her grandmother's lap and reached for the plate. "I think they're hungry," she told Stacy, inclining her head toward the booths. "They looked like they were fighting before. Maybe 'cause they were hungry. Daddy told me that people do bad things sometimes 'cause they don't have anything, and they're hungry. So I'll give that man my plate, and maybe he won't look like he's snarling all the time."

Shayne smiled, and he reminded himself that whatever agony and loss he felt over his marriage, Cindy was a good person, and a good mother, and between them, they'd created a couple of really good children.

Genevieve, the plate wobbling a little precariously in her hands, walked over and set it in front of Luke DeFeo.

He studied her for a long moment.

"Thanks, kid," he said.

The television screen flashed back into working order; local news was on.

"We expect snow at this time of year," a weatherman was saying, "but the intensity of the drifts that reached the mountains was higher than predicted. Plows are busy, and police and rescue agencies are out on the roads searching for those who started out for homes in the Blue Ridge area and didn't quite make it home for Christmas."

A cameraman was focused on a car that had slid into an embankment, precariously near the guardrail. From that area, if a car had gone over...

Shayne leaned forward, feeling as if his heart were caught in his throat.

It couldn't be. It couldn't be Cindy's Subaru! Cindy was on her way to Paris; she'd started seeing a travel agent when the divorce had been final and he'd been offered a freebie at a chalet in France. She'd been due to leave on Christmas Eve.

Of course, it couldn't be Cindy's car. There were thousands of Subaru Foresters in the area. They were good cars for harsh winters.

It was a moss-green Forester, just like his wife's car.

Ex-wife's car! he reminded himself.

Shayne glanced around quickly, wondering if the children were watching the screen; they weren't. Genevieve was still staring at Luke DeFeo, smiling, as if she admired him a great deal, and Connor was involved in his game.

He stared back at the television screen.

If there was a cameraman there, the driver and passengers, assuming there were any, had to be all right.

"It's an overhead shot," DeFeo said.

"What?"

"Look, it's an overhead shot. Must be a helicopter... Look how the shot shakes, zooming in and out."

He was right.

Shayne felt every muscle in his body tighten; he studied everything he could for the seconds that the waving shot remained on the screen. He searched for a sign of some kind that would tell him exactly where in the mountains the car was stranded.

He found it, right before the screen switched to a traffic pileup in Charlottesburg.

Dead Man's Curve.

It wasn't an official designation, and he wasn't sure just what mile marker it was in the Blue Ridge. It was about five miles down from them. He knew it from the overlook at the apron of the curve and the flat-face rock just to the side of it.

He stood, heedless of DeFeo. He walked over to the bar. Mac had paused to exchange a few words with his father.

"I don't know, and I don't know why, but I think that Cindy is stranded on the mountain, maybe freezing to death. Dad, I'm going down there."

Chapter 9

There would be no arguing with Shayne; Morwenna knew that.

Stacy, of course, was upset. Shayne might be a working physician in his mid-thirties and a father himself; he was still *her* child. Stacy was disturbed already—of course they all were—and now this new danger to her family seemed to be making her even more anxious. "But, Shayne, really—Cindy is supposed to be in Europe by now," Stacy said.

"There's no way you could know that you saw *Cindy's* car," Mike said.

"Look, I know exactly where the car was stuck," Shayne said. "You don't understand. I have a feeling. A gut feeling. And I know Cindy, and I know that she never knew these mountains like we do. She's probably in that car—maybe even injured. I have to go. I have to."

"I'll go with you," Morwenna said.

Both her parents gasped.

"No, Morwenna, let me go with Shayne," Bobby said.

She turned to look at her brother. "Look, Wenna, I'm not saying you're out of shape or anything. You're in great shape. But I do way more in the snow than you do. I'm a far better skier, I am much better with a snowboard and I'm even a better hiker."

"You can't take skis out there," Stacy said. "The snow is covering too many ruts…you won't always see the ledges—with the sun out, the snow can be blinding."

"And if you walked again, it could take forever," Mike said.

"I've got a snowmobile out back," Mac said. "She's not the newest model, but she's a workhorse. If you follow close to the road, you'll be safe enough in it."

"You have any survival kits?" Shayne asked him. "Bobby, don't make Mom and Dad worry for two. If Mac can lend me the snowmobile, I'll be there and back in no time."

"Hell, no," Bobby said. "I know the roads better than any of you. I'm the one who still spends the most time here."

"Kid!" Luke DeFeo called from the booth. "Your brother doesn't know that his wife is in any car stuck anywhere. She's in Europe. That car could belong to anyone. I understand how you feel, but you need to be sensible."

Morwenna looked at him. Could the man really be worried about her family?

Genevieve had been standing there, looking from adult to adult. She suddenly cried out and ran to her father. "Daddy, is Mommy out in the snow?"

Shayne shot Luke DeFeo a murderous stare. "No, darling, probably not. I'm just kind of a worrywart, you know that. I saw a car stuck that looks kind of like Mommy's."

Morwenna hadn't even seen Connor come over to stand behind his grandfather.

"It could be Mommy," he said. "She was crying before you came to get us yesterday morning, Dad. She wanted us to be with you, but she didn't want to be away from us."

Morwenna felt something behind her back and she turned around, startled. Gabe Lange had left his booth, and stood just behind her.

They were getting too lax! They needed to be watching him.

"Connor, I don't think that you have to worry. Your dad is a doctor, and I think he would have thought about getting to that car whether it's actually your mom in it or not. Whoever is stranded probably needs help," he said.

"I have to go," Shayne said quietly.

Stacy looked at her son for a long moment. "Yes, of course you do," she said.

"You realize," Luke DeFeo called from his booth. "Gabe wants two of the able-bodied men out of here because he's planning something. This could be a fool's errand; that car could have been stranded since last night, and whoever is in it is probably dead."

Genevieve started to sob. Stacy picked her up. "Honey, it could be someone else's car, and your mommy may be safe in a nice warm chalet some-where," she said.

"And there are two able-bodied men and a few strong boys here as well," Mac protested in a growl. "Shayne, there's a rescue kit on the back wall of the kitchen—take that. The snowmobile keys are right by it. You and Bobby get going. You'll be back here in no time, and you're going to want to be back before dark."

"We'll be here—Mac and my family and I," Brian Williamson said firmly. "Everything will be status quo."

"We'll be fine, won't we, Mom?" Morwenna said, setting an arm around her mother's shoulders.

"At least grab a piece of turkey before you leave," Stacy said, forcing a smile.

"All right, we're going," Shayne said. Genevieve came running over to hug his legs; Shayne picked her up and gave her a kiss on the cheek. "Don't you worry, munchkin. And Connor, you watch out for your sister for me, right?"

Connor nodded gravely.

The two grabbed their coats and headed around the bar to go out through the kitchen. Mike was staring worriedly after his sons; he held the shotgun in a lax position.

Morwenna turned to Gabe. "You! Back to the table," she told him.

"This worries me sick!" DeFeo said from his position in his booth. "They're on a fool's errand. The snow is blanketing all kinds of hazards. And," he said, looking directly at Morwenna, "your brother hates his ex-wife."

Genevieve gasped.

"You shut up, and shut up right now," Morwenna said, approaching the table. "One more word, and you may be the ghost of J. Edgar Hoover, but I'll knock you out flat with my rifle butt and not feel a twitch of guilt as I do it!" she warned.

There was an uncomfortable silence.

And they all heard the motor of the snowmobile start up and rev.

Morwenna looked from DeFeo to Gabe Lange, who had taken his seat again. He was watching her. He smiled when their eyes met. "They're going to be fine," he told her with assurance.

"Maybe," DeFeo said, sounding weary. He groaned. "I really wish you could see what's happening here. This man is being as nice as he can be. He's trying to make you all like him. He's pretending to be good and kind, and worried about you rather than himself. That's his act. He's seducing you all with his gentle personality. And then he'll strike."

They were all silent for a minute.

"Eat your turkey!" Stacy told him. "Before we lock you in the outhouse!"

DeFeo smiled. "There's an outhouse?"

"We can arrange for one," Mike assured him.

"I wish you'd let me help you," DeFeo said. "You're good people. I wish I could make you see what you're doing, and that you're being used, which puts you into a greater realm of danger."

Bobby was glad that Mac Scott was a real mountain man; his survival kit contained rope, carabiners, pulleys, water, bandages, water and medical supplies. His snowmobile had three compartments, and one held a heavy windbreaker and blanket, while another held flashlights and emergency flares.

He convinced his brother to sit behind him and let him do the steering; Shayne was feeling desperate, he knew, but his brother was never stupid. Bobby did know the mountain best.

Still, it was rough going. The snow was deep, and all discernible lines between the road itself, the embankment on the right and the guardrails on the left had all but disappeared.

Bobby kept the speed in check. At the best of

times, in a car with the world's finest tires, mountain roads could be treacherous. No one in their right mind would have been on the roads late yesterday; only those who really knew the mountain could have foreseen just how bad it was going to be.

Were they crazy? Was Cindy in Europe? Were they really on a fool's errand, whose only possible end would be to come across a corpse frozen in place behind the wheel?

And yet it was true; Shayne had panicked because of his ex-wife. But, if he had realized that he could reach the car and that it might be occupied, he would have come out anyway. No physician had ever taken his oath more seriously.

He was jarred from his thoughts as the snowmobile suddenly bounced high and slammed back down—he'd hit a rock or obstruction on the road. He heard Shayne swear, and felt his brother's arms tighten around him. When they landed, he cut his speed, slowing almost to a stop and shouting back at Shayne, "You okay?"

"Yeah, yeah, slow her down more, I guess," Shayne said.

"Can't save anyone if we're dead or broken," Bobby agreed.

He'd almost come to a stop; he revved the motor again, making sure to keep it alive as well. The snowy air hit his face with a fierce blast—stinging. He hugged the mountain as closely as he dared. They were on a road, damn it, but they might as well have been on a field of snow. Only the towering heights of the pines and evergreens on the mountainside gave him any sense of direction.

He should have grabbed a ski mask. He felt as if his nose was so cold, it was burning off.

He rounded bend after bend, and slowed as the slope became greater.

He blinked hard as his eyes watered at the cold air. He didn't dare look too far to the left; they could see the towns in the valley below, so far down that they looked like little houses in a Christmas display.

He focused on driving, and again, they curved down another bend.

And there they saw the moss-green Subaru,

slammed against the overhead, and the embankment, and far too close to the ledge.

If Morwenna had been feeling fraught with tension before, it was nothing compared to the way
she was feeling now. Shayne and Bobby were gone,
and from the time they left, she discovered that
she was looking up at the big, carved bear-framed
clock over the bar.

Seconds ticked by so slowly.

Brian and Mary Williamson and their boys had
been a godsend; Brian had gotten it into his head
to teach the boys how to play pool, and so he and
Mary—an excellent player herself—were distract-
ing them to the best of their ability. Stacy was
keeping Genevieve as busy as possible, having her
help out, putting down and picking up plates and
refilling beverage glasses.

Mac and Morwenna had gotten the rest of the
turkey dinners out, only everyone had seemed to
have lost their appetite. The boys ate a few bites
between shots; Morwenna played with her fork,
herself, pushing her food around on her plate.

Only their two prisoners seemed to clean up their turkey and stuffing, mashed potatoes and gravy, green beans and cranberry sauce.

They, too, seemed to be watching the clock.

It had seemed like forever before the day had begun—it was only four in the afternoon. Morwenna prayed that her brothers would return before the sun fell in earnest.

The TV had given nothing but static since it had last gone out.

"Hey!" Gabe called to her softly.

She narrowed her eyes, looking at him. It was best, she'd decided, to keep away from both the men. Gabe had thought immediately that Shayne and Bobby should risk their own lives. DeFeo had openly voiced the thought that if it was Cindy in the stranded car, she might well be dead.

"Is that a jukebox? A working one?" he asked her.

She looked down past the pool tables.

"Yes, it still works."

"Maybe it has some Christmas carols," he said. "May I go look?"

Morwenna looked at her father. Mike now maintained an iron grasp around the shotgun.

Her father shrugged. Stacy looked up; Genevieve was on her lap and they were drawing pictures on a cocktail napkin.

"Go ahead. And, remember, Dad *will* shoot you if you make a wrong move," Morwenna said.

Gabe eased himself out of the booth and headed down past the pool players. For a moment, Morwenna feared that she had been an idiot; Gabe could have stopped by one of the boys, slipped his bound wrists over the head of one of them and threatened to strangle him. He could have then threatened a life...using a child as a hostage to escape.

She pictured the scene in her mind's eye, and she almost cried out in fear and warning. But she saw that her father had no intention of risking the children. He had risen, and though Gabe couldn't see him, Mike had kept himself in a position to shoot if Gabe had made so much as a move in the wrong direction.

Gabe walked right by the pool players and down to the jukebox.

He looked back at her with a rueful smile. "It works off of quarters."

"Here!" Mac spoke up from behind the bar and opened the cash register to find a handful of coins; he handed them to Morwenna. She met his eyes, and he nodded. "Lord knows, we could use something in here beyond the sound of that TV static," he said.

Morwenna walked down to the jukebox with the coins in her hand. When she reached it, she began to feed them into the machine.

"You all have to be careful," DeFeo said.

"I am careful—always," Mike told him.

Gabe was able to hit the button that changed the pages.

"A17. Nice, Bing Crosby and David Bowie singing together, 'Little Drummer Boy' and 'Peace on Earth,'" he said.

"You're letting him run the show!" DeFeo warned.

"He's choosing a few Christmas tunes. A nice idea, really," Morwenna said.

"So, I'm stuck here in cuffs with a group that is going to be in big trouble when the real law arrives. But we all get to play Christmas tunes. Great!"

She opted to ignore DeFeo.

"Play what you choose," Morwenna said.

Gabe hit A17 without answering DeFeo. He flipped more pages. Morwenna was startled when Genevieve called out "Do they have 'Rudolph the Red-Nosed Reindeer'?"

"Well, I'll just bet they do," Gabe told her. "And there it is! D22!"

"I'd like 'Do You Hear What I Hear?'" Stacy called.

"And there's the ever-popular 'Rockin' Around the Christmas Tree'!" Mike called from the bar.

He was still seated on his stool, still clutching the shotgun. What a contrast to Genevieve, who wasn't questioning what she believed in any way. She simply liked Gabe.

The faith of a child…

Gabe began to push buttons. As he did so, Morwenna stepped back to join the boys gathered around the pool table. Connor grinned up at her; she realized that although he was still worried about his parents and aware of the tense situation in which the family found itself, he was doing all right.

Friends had made that so—learning pool tricks from the Williamson family was easing the day for him.

She smiled back at him. "A budding pool shark, eh?" she teased affectionately.

He smiled back at her. "My dad…my dad is going to be okay, right, Auntie Wenna?" he asked.

She saw that Gabe was still listening and obeying as the group in the tavern vied for selections on the old jukebox. His eyes were alight.

She had been suspicious of the man from the beginning. Then she had begun to believe in him. Then she had found her way back to mistrust. And why? Because someone else spoke against him.

She winced. Well, that hadn't stood history very

well. Proof was needed. Well, proof was what they awaited.

"You dad is going to be just fine, Connor," Morwenna said. "And so are we."

But just as the words left her mouth, the electricity went.

And the tavern was pitched into shadow.

Bobby braked the snowmobile just off the point where he *thought* the road made way for the lookout point. Shayne dismounted and instantly started for the car.

"Bro! We have to be careful. That car is right on the ledge," Bobby told him.

Shayne froze in his tracks, as if at his statement, and Bobby saw that his face was white. And then he knew why. He couldn't see that it was indeed Cindy in the car, but he could see the driver.

And the driver was in a hooded parka, head down on the steering wheel. Frost and snow covered most of the windshield.

There was no way to tell, until they touched the driver, whether the person was alive or dead.

"All right, come on, Shayne, I want to bring you both—and me!—back alive. Let's take it slow." He reached into the side compartments on the snowmobile. He got out the rope and the pulley chair, and followed Shayne as his brother more cautiously approached the car. He saw one of the huge light poles by the side of the road. It wouldn't carry the weight of a car if something happened, but it would carry the weight of a man—and a woman.

"Approach the car, and carefully open that front door just in case the ground by the back tires is— is gone. Grab the person out of the car, and screw whatever the hell else is in it, okay?" Bobby said. "I'll tie us together with the rope."

Shayne nodded. "Let's hurry," he said.

Bobby took the rope to the massive light stand and quickly tied it around, securing it with double loops. He hurried back to where his brother stood, already securing himself. He looked at Bobby. "Thanks," he told him.

"I'll be right here, but not coming close. Until she's out of the car, and you need me," Bobby said.

His brother moved toward the car then, taking every step carefully.

Bobby looked back at the rope attached to the giant light pole, and then frowned as he looked up at the light. Dusk was settling on them more heavily now with each minute that passed.

And the streetlight hadn't kicked on.

Strange, the lights usually came on automatically as dusk moved in.

Unless, of course, the electricity had finally gone in the mountaintops here.

And, if so, back at the tavern, his family was locked in darkness.

Bobby forced himself to remain still, to watch his brother, and to wait. He couldn't go screaming like a terrified child, and rush back to the snowmobile and leave Shayne and the driver.

What if the woman was Cindy, and she had skidded and lost control last night, and she had frozen to death already?

He didn't dare think it.

What about his family, back in the tavern, suddenly pitched into darkness?

His father was a smart man; he'd have his shotgun at the ready.

But could he aim in the dark?

"Almost there," Shayne called to him. "And the ground feels steady thus far…don't know about the back, and I'm not going to test it."

Shayne stood then by the driver's-side door. He reached for it slowly, and opened it more slowly. He let out a cry as the driver slumped to the side, and into his arms. He fell to his knees, cradling the woman in his arms.

Bobby heard a strange sound; it was like a rumble, but it was a quiet rumbling. He looked at the Subaru, and the back end of it seemed to be sinking.

"Shayne, get her out of there!" Bobby shouted. He went for the rope, ready to drag his brother if it went taut against the pole.

But Shayne stood, cradling his ex-wife to his chest, and he started a stumbling run through the snow toward Bobby. And as he did, Bobby heard a creaking sound, once and again, and then growing louder, and he saw that the Subaru was slipping, slipping...

There was a loud smashing sound as it hit the guardrail, and then a rumble as it burst through the railing and went tumbling down the mountain.

"Brace yourself!" Bobby said, hunkering down.

And Shayne dropped to a knee, covering Cindy's body with his own. They both waited for an explosion.

None came.

Bobby stood slowly and walked as close as he dared to the ledge. He looked over, and he was glad to see that the Subaru had not exploded, or hurt anything other than a number of scraggly, half-dead winter trees and brush. It had landed—right side up—on a narrow ledge about fifty feet down.

He looked at Shayne. His brother had gotten Cindy to the snowmobile; he had her wrapped in the blanket, and he was trying to urge some brandy through her lips. Bobby hurried over to them, falling to his knees in the snow, and looking down at his sister-in-law's face. She was such a beautiful woman, but right now, he felt a burst of cold fear sweep through him. She was so white; her eyes were closed, and her lips appeared to be a strange shade of blue.

"She's—she's—" Bobby began.

Shayne smiled grimly at him. "She's alive," he assured her. "She's...she's a fighter. She's going to make it. Her pulse is weak, but steady. She's going to come around. We just have to get her back as soon as possible, and get her warm...and I can find out if any damage was done. She should get to a hospital, but the tavern will do. I need her to come around...to sip some of this."

Bobby felt words coming in a repetitious prayer. *Let her live, let her live, please, God, let her live.*

"Come on, come on, come on...please, God!" Shayne breathed.

Cindy suddenly choked, coughed and stuttered.

Her eyes flew open in panic, and she strained at the arms that held her: Shayne's.

A weak scream escaped her lips, and then died as her eyes focused on Shayne's face.

"Shayne!" she said.

"Hey," Shayne said, his voice tremulous. "You're all right. You're all right."

Was she? Bobby wondered. God knew, she might be suffering from some kind of frostbite.

She saw Bobby then. "Bobby!" she whispered. "My God, you two found me...how on earth did you find me? You couldn't have known that I was coming. I didn't know that I was coming until it was time to leave for the airport, and then I knew I—I knew I couldn't leave for the whole week, and I tried to call you all, but no one was answering and I just took a chance, and, oh, Lord, please forgive me, Shayne... I meant to get here and beg that you all forgive me for showing up so rudely, and let me spend the holidays with the kids, too, and—"

"Cindy, you may be suffering some real effects from this," Shayne said gently. "Drink a bit more of this, and let me get you some water, too. We'll wrap you up really tightly in the parka, because it's even colder when we're on the snowmobile. It will be slow going...the thing is only meant for two, but I know that we'll manage. The tavern is warm, and once we're there, we'll talk."

"But, Shayne, I asked you to take the children, and I came here, and then…I thought I was going to die. I was terrified to move in the car." She stopped speaking and stared at Bobby. "The car, I was in the car…"

Shayne looked at him. "Um, well, it's standing. But I have a feeling the insurance company might consider it to be totaled," Bobby said.

"Oh! Oh, God! It did go over! I was terrified when the car spun out and stalled, and then when the wheels wouldn't catch. There was nothing for them to catch on!"

"It's okay, Cindy, you're safe," Shayne said.

"Shayne, you risked your life for me," Cindy said, her eyes filled with wonder as she looked at him. "After everything…but, it's what you do, isn't it?" Her eyes filled with tears.

Shayne drew her to him.

"Cindy, don't cry. Please, don't cry."

"But you forgive me?" she whispered.

"Forgive you? For loving our children? Don't

be silly, Cindy, there is nothing to forgive. And you will always be a part of the family, and always welcome," Shayne said.

"And we'll all freeze if we don't get back," Bobby interjected.

He glanced at the light pole, and far up—at the light that wasn't lit.

Cindy was alive.

And now, the worry that something had gone wrong at the tavern began to eat into him again.

"We need to hurry, as much as we safely can," Shayne said.

Screw safely!

Bobby's urge to get back to the tavern was almost overwhelming. He began hurriedly gathering the equipment they had used, stuffing it into the compartments. He crawled back onto the snowmobile and felt Shayne doing his best to get on with his ex-wife in his arms.

"What is it? What's wrong?" Cindy asked.

Where in the hell did they begin to explain?

He'd leave that to Shayne, Bobby decided.

He turned on the snowmobile's lights—a contrast to the darkness now settling heavy on the mountains.

The cold hit Bobby's face as he revved the snow-mobile into gear; going back would be even more treacherous.

He kept seeing the pool of light before him.

And all he could think was *dark, dark, dark.*

His family was trapped in the dark, with strangers whose intentions were still unknown.

Chapter 10

The sudden darkness seemed complete at first; the sun was almost down outside the tavern walls, and the shadowy world of the outside was now inside, compounded by the walls surrounding them.

But it wasn't completely dark.

There was that moment when it was just suddenly dead silent, smoke gray, and dead still, and yet shapes and shadows seemed to run amok.

They were frightened, of course; man's fear of the dark

was an instinct left over from prehistory when darkness meant the coming of fearsome beasts of prey.

Morwenna wasn't sure at all why such stark terror came to her. It wasn't unusual that they should lose the electricity. Mac had a generator, and it would kick in soon. But she had the strangest feeling that *this* sudden darkness was worse than any other, and that something evil was moving about the room. Light couldn't come back to them fast enough.

Something almost touched her, and for a moment, she felt as if her skin was literally crawling, as if a horrible scent of death, decay and sulfur filled the air.

She reached for Genevieve, terrified that the little girl was in some kind of danger. She groped blindly, watching shadows move.

"Hey, folks, it's okay, everything's all right now. We've got an emergency generator," Mac said.

As if on cue, low light returned to the tavern, and the jukebox spun into action. Bing Crosby and David Bowie came on together.

Morwenna looked instantly for her niece; she

was standing beside and slightly behind Gabe, almost wedged against the jukebox. She had a wide-eyed look of fear on her face.

"Baby, it's okay," Morwenna said. "It's all right, see, the light is back on."

"Auntie Wenna, I was scared!" Genevieve said.

Morwenna quickly hunkered down by her side.

"It's all right. It was just dark," Morwenna said.

But Genevieve shook her head. "No, didn't you feel it...someone was here, someone very, very bad!"

"Genevieve, no one else is here. It was just a matter of moments before the lights came back on."

Genevieve looked up at her. "No! No, Gabe saved me. He saved me from the bad thing, the evil thing that was here."

"Hey!" Mike said suddenly.

Morwenna quickly glanced to her father. He had jumped up first, apparently to look for his family members, and to assure himself that they were all right.

"What?" Mac asked.

"He's gone!" Mike said.

Morwenna looked to the booth where Luke DeFeo had been sitting.

It was empty.

She quickly looked around the room. DeFeo wasn't anywhere to be seen.

She had the uneasy feeling that he had been near; that he had nearly touched her.

And Genevieve.

"Well, hell, maybe that's just good riddance!" Mac said.

"I didn't hear or see the door open," Connor noted, frowning.

"Well, he is gone," Stacy said. "Maybe—maybe it is just as well."

Gabe spoke up suddenly. "No, no, it's not just as well. He's still out there somewhere. And he's dangerous."

"Dangerous? But," Morwenna said, turning to him, "*you* said that he was a white-collar criminal. He said that *you* were the dangerous one."

He shook his head. "You don't understand… you can't understand. He's—all right, he's on the run. And he may want to bring a few down with him. You have to let me go after him."

He walked around the pool table, toward Mike. As he did so, Morwenna noticed the distance from the booths and around the pool table to where she was standing.

Luke DeFeo couldn't have come around the whole place so quickly. Could he? And yet she had the uncomfortable, uncanny feeling that he had.

"But—he's out there, alone in the snow. He won't be coming back here," Mac said.

"He's out there, and he's thinking of something, and he will come back," Gabe said firmly.

"My sons are out there," Stacy said. "My sons are out there, somewhere on the mountain."

"I can find him. I can stop him," Gabe said. "Look, please. I was with you for a long time, and no harm came to you. Trust me. Let me go after him, before he finds a way to hurt anyone. Please."

A silence followed his words. Thoughts raced through Morwenna's mind.

There was simply no way to know the truth; maybe Luke DeFeo had escaped because he was desperate to

*find a way to communicate with the law. Maybe he had
escaped because he was a cop, and he was going to come
back.*

And maybe every word that Gabe was saying
was the truth. He'd done nothing but show them
gratitude and kindness since he'd been with him.

She stepped forward, coming to stand behind
him. "I think we need to believe in Gabe. He's
been nothing but level and kind—he risked his
life for Genevieve, and I don't care what DeFeo
said—Gabe risked his life, and you don't do that
unless there is something really decent in you. He
wants to set out to find Luke DeFeo. I say we let
him go, and I say that I go with him."

"What?" Stacy said incredulously, sliding off her
bar stool to stare at her daughter.

"Mom, I'm well over twenty-one," she said quietly.

"No, I should go," Mike said.

Morwenna shook her head. "No, Dad. You and
Mom need to stay. You need to be here, because
you're really great parents." She paused, looking
at Genevieve and Connor, not wanting to scare

the children, but hoping her parents would understand.

If something had happened to Shayne, Bobby or Cindy—and something was to happen to her, God forbid!—the kids would need stable, loving parents.

And that, she realized, *they were.*

She smiled suddenly. "Gabe will never hurt me. I know it. I know it just as I know the sun will rise in the morning. And I'm going to untie his hands, and we're going to go out together. When we reach Shayne and Bobby, I'll come back with them. But they have to know that DeFeo is out there, and he could be very dangerous. We can't accomplish that with one person—I'll need to come back, and Gabe will need to find DeFeo."

"Now, wait, I can go out with this man," Brian Williamson said.

"Or me," Mac volunteered.

"I'll be able to find my brothers. I know that I'll be able to find my brothers," Morwenna said.

"This is crazy!" Mike said, still studying her.

"It's what we need to do, Dad. Mr. Williamson, you need to stay with your kids. And Mac, well, you just need to watch out for everyone here. And I need to find my brothers, and Gabe needs to stop DeFeo," Morwenna said firmly.

"And my mommy!" Genevieve said. "You need to find my mommy!"

"If she's with them," Morwenna said.

"She is," Connor said. "She is. My father went to find her. He *knew* that she was out there, and he went to find her. And I know that he did."

"Morwenna!" Her father lowered his head. "Morwenna, we just don't *know!*"

But Genevieve came to stand next to Morwenna and Connor. "I know!" she said. "I know that Gabe is good, and that he can find my daddy. Gramps, please, let him go, and let Auntie Morwenna go with him to bring my mommy and daddy and Uncle Bobby back."

Her father stared at her. She didn't know if he was thinking that he couldn't really stop her, or if he was feeling the same way; *they had to be right about Gabe Lange.* He nodded slowly. "You're taking my only daughter out there," he said to Gabe.

"I'll be careful with her," Gabe promised. "I swear to you, I would lay down my life for her."

Genevieve tugged on Morwenna's shirt, and Morwenna hunkered down to her. Genevieve looked at her with a child's wide eyes and then reached out to touch the little gold angel she was wearing around her neck.

"You'll be protected. You have your angel."

Morwenna smiled.

Faith, again.

Children could be so amazing. And it could be argued that faith could lead to stupidity, and that fanatical faith could lead to horrible things, but this wasn't that kind of faith. There was something in Gabe Lange's eyes unlike anything she had ever known before.

He made her believe.

She walked across the tavern, collecting her coat and gloves and scarf.

"We'll be back before you know it!" she assured the room cheerfully.

"Wait!" Mike protested. "You're just walking out with nothing—"

"We'll find Bobby and Shayne and the equipment. Dad, I know this mountain, and the valleys. We'll find them soon—I know it. I'm good, I'm fine. Have faith in me!"

Mike looked into her eyes. He smiled slowly and painfully. "I do have faith in you," he said.

Gabe followed her, and turned back. "You are going to be all right, and so are the others. I will find DeFeo. And I will stop him."

Bobby drove the snowmobile slowly and carefully; even so, the air was biting, and bits and chips of snow and ice flew before them and around them. Shayne's face was numb.

And yet, he felt a sense of wonder as they moved through the snow.

He had never been a violent man in any way, and certainly not with his wife or children. But when he looked back, he could see the danger signs that had led to his divorce. He had been oblivious to the amount of time he was gone—he felt that his days had been full from beginning to end. He *had* changed diapers. In fact, when trying to explain why she was leaving, Cindy had told him that he'd been a wonderful father when the kids had been babies. He was still a wonderful father.

He had tried to understand when she'd told him that she'd rather be alone on her own than always alone with him. That hadn't made sense. Not then. He'd been perplexed; he didn't go to strip bars, he didn't head out on wild nights looking for something new, hoping to get lucky with an exotic stranger.

But she hadn't thought that, apparently.

And he hadn't seen it coming, and when he did, it had been too late. She hadn't been angry; she had told him that she just didn't know him anymore, and he certainly didn't know her. And it was better to be alone, going about life on her own schedule than wondering what his might be, or if and when they were going to see him. Maybe if she wasn't always on the spot, he'd show up for his son's baseball games, or realize that Connor was falling in love with music, much like his uncle

Bobby, who would really stop and listen to him at times.

Now, of course, it was all so clear.

He still loved his wife.

He was certain that even if she had fallen out of love with him, she still cared about him.

And his hold on her was firm; he realized at that moment, as long as he had breath in his body there was hope, and if they never made it back together again, he was desperately glad that she was alive. She was a wonderful person, and an exceptional mother, and thank God, no matter what they chose to do themselves in the future, they were lucky—they knew how to be family.

Cindy moved slightly in his arms, wedged between him and Bobby on the snowmobile. She looked up at him, and she smiled.

She didn't try to speak, the snowmobile was making far too much noise.

He wished he could try to explain; he had been indignant, so certain that he had done nothing wrong.

And he hadn't. He just hadn't been there.

But the way that she looked at him then…

He brought his lips as close to her as possible, and whispered against the roar of the motor, "Cindy, I…don't ever feel that you have to…to look at me that way or be too grateful… I mean, I know I wronged you, and I'm just so grateful that you're alive!"

"I *feel* alive right now," she told him. "And I feel that I'm *with* you as I haven't been in forever, Shayne."

He started to lean his head against hers. Then he heard his brother shout over the loud *whir* of the snowmobile. "Almost there! Just one more bend!"

Shayne nodded. He moved his head enough to smile at Cindy.

"The kids will think that you're the best Christmas present ever," he told her.

She smiled.

Then Shayne heard Bobby shout, "What the hell?"

He slowed the snowmobile, but too late.

They hit something again, something buried beneath the white drifts.

And the snowmobile veered to the side—thankfully inward, toward the mountain—but then it careened into the pines, cracked against a tree and overturned.

"You know where you're going, right?" Gabe asked Morwenna.

She looked at him; it was bitterly cold. They'd already made the walk down, and made it through the snow. But it seemed that the going was rougher now. It was difficult to make sure that she was staying on the road, and it seemed that here, even more so than higher, the snow had collected in deeper piles.

She shrugged with a sheepish smile. "Down," she told him. She added anxiously, "They should be getting back up toward us, but I keep thinking we should hear the motor of that snowmobile— it's old, and it's loud."

"We'll catch up with them soon," he said.

"And how do you know that? And aren't you looking for DeFeo—not my family?" she asked him.

He looked ahead, and there was something grim in his expression.

Morwenna gasped. "You think that DeFeo is after my brothers! But, why? Why would he be after my brothers? Why wouldn't he just want to escape?"

"He wants to use them," Gabe said after a minute.

"Use them? As hostages? Gabe, he's unarmed, and my brothers aren't exactly puny!"

"He has his ways." Gabe looked at her then and sighed. "There are many things that you can steal from someone that aren't really tangible."

"That made no sense! What could he steal from my brothers?" she asked.

"Sorry," he said. "He might be after something extremely tangible—like the snowmobile."

She kept looking at him; he had changed his mind—regarding what he might have said to her.

"Gabe, what are you really trying to say?" she asked, and her concentration was so hard on his face as she tried to read what was behind his passive expression that she stumbled and fell into him, bringing them both down into the snow.

"I'm sorry," she breathed, pressing her gloved hands into the biting snow to rise above him, blushing.

He shook his head. "It's fine," he said. He stared up at her for a long moment, and there was something of wonder in his eyes, and then he sighed. "We need to move," he told her.

He laughed, getting his footing, and helping her to find hers once again.

"We've got to keep walking," he told her.

"We'll freeze," she agreed. "And we have to find them."

"We will find them."

"You're so sure!"

"Ah, well, you see," he said lightly, "I believe in Christmas, for all that it means."

"You're not talking about a lit tree and ornaments, are you?" Morwenna said, smiling at him. "You are sunshine and light," she added dryly.

"Ah, well, I know that it's sometimes hard to see, and often impossible to understand, but I do believe in a greater power, and I may be a cop, but I do believe that *most* people are inherently good. We have basic needs, and then we have wants… and then we have desires. We're easily hurt, and when we're hurt, we're defensive, and we lash out. There really are seven sins, you know," he said lightly.

"And we all, in some way or another, fall into them all?" she asked.

"Not all of us into *all* of them," he said, grinning. "And," he added, "Christmas Day is special in many ways. You know—if you're a kid, you wait for Santa. If you're Christian, you believe in celebrating the birth of the man who taught us that we could be saved from all the bad we can fall into because we are human. No matter how people see their faith, the world is really one big family, and they say, too, that it's a family above and below the world as well."

"Heaven and hell?" Morwenna asked him.

He grinned. "Think of it all as one big family. Except there was one child who was very, very bad in his behavior. He envied his sisters and his brothers, and he envied every other creature, certain that everyone and everything was loved more than he was. And so let's say his parent sent him to stand in the corner, and while he was standing in the corner, he plotted a zillion other ways to get into trouble—and to get others to get into trouble with him. Now, as badly as he might be behaving, like any child, he's still loved. But his brothers and sisters have to look after him all the time, and make sure that he doesn't hurt others or get them into trouble with him."

Morwenna stared at him incredulously. She laughed softly. "Okay, so we're all one big family. God and man and—"

"All the angels," he told her. "Those who are well behaved, and, of course, the brother who just can't seem to behave. But, you see, here's the good thing—as bad as things look, and as bad as they are at times, we do have Christmas, when we celebrate the fact that good will outweigh what's bad. Belief is the hardest thing in the world…belief in what's intangible, and belief in ourselves."

Morwenna looked ahead, and she didn't know

why, but she was suddenly reminded of the scene she had seen on television. Mexico. Over a hundred million strong—and a country with tons of tourist cities. But Alex had managed to get himself captured—with Double-D Debbie—for a few seconds on camera. She had been hurt, yes. Hurt—or had she felt humiliated? Or was it both? Of course she felt hurt. *But had she known? Had she realized, when they couldn't come to an agreement over the holiday, that there was something that...that just wasn't there?*

And if she was so hurt, why didn't she feel it now?

Because she loved her brothers; her brothers loved her. And they were out there somewhere.

She turned and looked at Gabe and laughed. "You are one crazy policeman, you know?"

He shrugged. "Maybe. But I'm also a very lucky one today."

"Why is that?"

"I happened upon people who prove the point that decency and goodness can so often win out. Miss MacDougal, I do indeed rest my point!"

She shook her head, smiling.

"If we find them," she whispered then.

"We will," he assured her.

"How can you be so certain that everything will be all right?" she demanded.

"Because of you, right now. Because I know that you won't stop until you find them."

She laughed again, with a dry note in her voice. "No, you don't know the mountains. Terrible things happen so easily. There are high ridges that fall straight down a thousand feet. When there's weather, there are horrible potholes that can wreck almost any kind of vehicle. And there's treacherous ice. And the weather is so cold—we can all freeze on the mountain."

He smiled at her again. "Well, then, I will have been privileged to have known you all."

She met his eyes, and she felt oddly warm and certain despite the cold. "No," she said softly. "I think we have been privileged to have known you."

He looked back at her for a long moment.

"Look!" Gabe pointed out. "Look—there are some tracks, and something…"

"Something what?" Morwenna demanded.

"Something heavy was dragged through the snow," Gabe said.

And it had been. There was a flattened path of ground ahead of them.

"Hurry!" Gabe said, and he started ahead of her, somehow making tremendous speed across the slick ground.

And then it seemed that the world around them groaned, as if there was a crack of thunder that had split the sky. The sound echoed and ricocheted through the trees.

"What…?" Morwenna began.

"He's found them," Gabe said grimly. "DeFeo has found your brothers."

Bobby had felt himself lose control; it had been like spinning on black ice…no, he had been spinning, but it's because they had hit something beneath the snow that shouldn't have been there.

The impact of the vehicle had shuddered down the length of him.

And then he'd landed in the snow, and for a moment, he was aware only of the cold, the feel of the air and the pain in his body. There was something on top of him. The world was white...

He was pinned beneath the snowmobile.

"Shayne!" He cried his brother's name. "Cindy!"

"Yeah, yeah..." Shayne said. "Cindy, Cindy..."

He felt his brother trying to scramble around him, pulling his ex-wife from the wreckage.

"Is she all right?" Bobby asked.

"I'm—I'm okay!" Cindy said.

"Bobby?" Shayne asked, rushing to his side.

"I can't—I can't get out," Bobby said.

"Can you feel your legs, can you move them?" Shayne demanded.

His brother was there, down on his knees in the snow, next to him. Bobby tried to wiggle his toes and move his ankles. He didn't think that anything was broken; he was just stuck.

"Yes, yes, I can move everything," Bobby said.

Shayne nodded. "All right, I'm going to try to

move the snowmobile. And when I do, you have to wriggle out quickly."

"Gotcha."

"Shayne, what do I do?" Cindy asked.

"You can try to add your weight when I lift," Shayne told her. "Ready?"

Cindy stood by him, ready to lift.

But though Shayne was strong, and had Cindy's help, the weight of the snowmobile was just too much.

"Listen, you two just get back to the tavern," Bobby said, forcing cheerfulness into his voice. "Get help, and get back here."

"I'm not leaving you like this," Shayne told him.

"Hey, Shayne!" Bobby protested. "We can't all just stay here—where will that get us?"

"I'm going to get a pulley system going…we've still got the rope. Cindy, you should probably be in a hospital, but can you take the rope—you remember how to do the knots, right?"

"Of course," Cindy said. "Hey, I didn't spend time with Dad for nothing! I mean, your father," she amended quickly. "I've got it. I'm really all right, Shayne, I can help. Give me the rope."

"All right," Shayne said, pausing and looking around. "There...walk over there. That tree looks good and sturdy and it's at the right angle...take that end of the rope, Cindy, and make sure it's a good knot."

Bobby heard the snow crunching as Cindy hurried off to do as she had been instructed. He watched as Shayne studied the snowmobile and the way it had fallen and then started to loop the heavy nylon rope around the snowmobile. "With the tree helping to create a lever system, we will get this thing up in no time," Shayne promised him.

Bobby was able to grab his brother's ankle. Shayne looked down at him.

"If you don't get this up now," Bobby said sternly, "you're going to take Cindy to the tavern, get Dad and Mac and come back for me."

"I'm going to get it up. What, are you kidding me? Can you imagine Mom if I come back without you? Don't worry—I'm going to manage this!" Shayne told him. "Cindy—"

Shayne went dead still, and quiet. Bobby tried to twist around and see what was going on; he couldn't.

He could only see his brother's face, and his features were knotted in a look of wary dread.

"What?" Bobby whispered.

But Shayne didn't look down at him.

Bobby heard someone else speaking, and he knew the voice.

Luke DeFeo.

"That's right, I have the pretty little ex-missus!" DeFeo said. "And nothing is going to happen to her. As long as you all play it right. I want that snowmobile. You're going to get it up and running, and then everything will be fine."

Bobby strained and twisted, trying to see around the snowmobile. He managed to wriggle enough to look around the front; Luke DeFeo had Cindy in a choke hold against his body.

"I know what I'm doing," he said quietly. "One

wrong move and her neck snaps. And I still get the snowmobile. Are we clear?"

"Perfectly," Shayne said, ice in his words.

Bobby saw DeFeo smile. "Don't worry. I let her get a good knot on that rope before I nabbed her. Dr. MacDougal, now it's all up to you and your brother there. I want the snowmobile up, and I want it running, and when it is, I'll take your ex with me just down the road a hair, and I'll leave her for you gentlemen to find again."

Cindy was staring at Shayne, tears in her eyes. Bobby knew why she hadn't screamed; she was flat against DeFeo's back, and his arm was in a hold that prevented her from uttering so much as a squeak. She looked at Shayne with apology in her eyes, and fear that she couldn't quite hide.

Cindy hadn't even known about DeFeo! She hadn't known anything about the strange night that had passed, or about the stranger day that had followed…

The darkness was beginning to settle around them in earnest.

And with the darkness would come a greater cold.

"I have to get to the tree with the lever," Shayne

said. "I'm moving, and I'm going to need to be there. I'm going to get the snowmobile off my brother, and we'll get it up together. Don't do anything. I'll get you the damn snowmobile."

"Fine. Do it," DeFeo said.

Something of a little squeak did escape Cindy as DeFeo jerked her back and away from the tree.

Bobby cursed himself for getting stuck beneath the snowmobile. If he had just realized what could have happened, if he'd have tried to jump clear...

Bobby saw as Shayne moved, delving first into the storage compartment for the lever. He then heard his brother's footsteps crunching through the snow as he headed for the tree.

He could barely see Shayne anymore, and DeFeo was caught in the crazy light that emanated from the headlight of the snowmobile. There was something not quite right about the man.

He could hear Shayne, struggling with the pulley system he was trying to assemble and work with the tree and the rope. His brother, he thought, had it rigged, and he was using all his strength to pull.

The snowmobile seemed to ease up on Bobby; he tried to slip out.

His brother let out a grunt, having to stop for a minute.

"Or," DeFeo said quietly, "you could leave me to deal with this. Take the little lady up to the tavern—and leave me here with your brother. What a fix! Desert your baby brother. What should you do, Shayne? You've got about two more minutes to move that snowmobile, or I'll take charge in the way that I see fit."

"I'm not leaving anyone!" Shayne snapped.

"Then you'd better get going, right?" DeFeo warned.

Shayne faced him. "Really? Aren't you a bit of a fool? The minute you release Cindy, we'll all be right on top of you, you lying bastard!"

Bobby winced. He wasn't sure that threatening the man was the way to go. But Shayne wasn't going to leave him, and he wasn't going to let the man hurt Cindy. He was testing Shayne, trying to make him decide between the mother of his children and his brother.

"What do you care about the woman?" DeFeo asked him. "Didn't she leave you? Didn't she walk out on you, screw around with some other man using the money you worked for? The bitch is only here now because she couldn't stand you having her children."

"If you hurt her," Shayne said, "you will be a dead man."

DeFeo started to laugh. Bobby blinked. He looked so strange in the glow that was cast by the headlight. He seemed bigger than he had been. He seemed to radiate a strange smell so powerful that it even reached Bobby where he lay, caught beneath the heavy snowmobile.

It was something like the scent of...brimstone!

"Boy, where's the Hippocratic oath now?" DeFeo said. "Well, Mr. Moralist, you'll have to figure out something here, won't you? Your brother or your ex-wife, the precious mother of your precocious little brats!"

"I'll get you the snowmobile!" Shayne said.

"Oh, I don't know," DeFeo said. "Maybe I'll just take her with me all the way..."

His hold on Cindy must have eased a fraction.

She cried out, "Shayne, don't let him hurt Bobby, don't—"

The sound strangled as he clenched his arm more tightly around her.

Dear God, Bobby prayed. *What do we do, what can I say, how—*

He was suddenly aware of a rush of sound. And suddenly, Cindy was almost flying toward him in the snow.

DeFeo cried out in surprise.

And Bobby realized that someone had come up behind DeFeo; they had all been so intent on the interaction between them that none of them had heard a thing.

They hadn't seen a thing...

But someone had come.

Gabe Lange.

Morwenna ran as fast behind Gabe as she could. Following him, she had first gone dead still in horror. The snowmobile was on its side...on top of someone!

And then, of course, she had seen DeFeo's back. And she had realized that he was holding someone in a death grip. And she hadn't even had time to think.

Gabe had taken off.

And then he was on DeFeo's back.

She heard a scream, and it came from Cindy, who had been thrust forward, falling into a massive drift. While Gabe attacked DeFeo from behind, DeFeo reached around, shouting out in rage, grabbing at Gabe.

Morwenna raced toward the trees, finding a stick. She ran around in front of the grappling men and began thrashing hard at DeFeo with her haphazard weapon. He lashed out with a fist, and he struck her in the chest. She was stunned at the blow; it sent her flying back hard into the trees. She was aware of Shayne rushing by her, ready to join the attack, and then she was aware of Shayne again, flying by her as if he weighed no more than an Easter bunny.

She heard Bobby, roaring in frustration, unable to help. She saw that Cindy was up, crawling over toward Bobby, and that Shayne was trying to rise, shaking his head, as if he could clear it.

She scrambled to her feet and looked around for a weapon. There was a huge tree branch by her feet and she went for it, and then charged in again, whacking at DeFeo—trying to make sure that she missed Gabe.

Except that she didn't miss him; she caught him in the arm. He bellowed, but he didn't even seem to notice her, so intent was he on DeFeo.

"Give it up! Give it up!" Gabe raged to DeFeo. "I've won. You're done here, you're done here! Give it up!"

Shayne charged in again, going for DeFeo's legs. He toppled the man, but Gabe went down, too. Morwenna grabbed her branch, trying again to get a good crack in on DeFeo's head.

She aimed well, and this time, she hit him.

She *knew* that she hit him.

But he didn't even notice. Even though the sound seemed like a shot in the cold air, *it didn't even faze him.*

She went to strike again, but to her amazement, both men were up.

"You've lost!" Gabe shouted again. "You've lost!"

But DeFeo didn't want to give up the fight. His face was contorted in a hideous mask of rage, and he stared at Gabe, as if he *knew* somewhere he had been defeated, but he just couldn't accept that it might be so. He was going to lunge at Gabe again, but then another sound seemed to rip apart the crisp air and the icy mountaintop.

A roll of thunder. There was no lightning, there was no sign of a coming storm...

But the sky suddenly lit up as if the earth had spun crazily toward the sun for one bizarre moment; then the sound of thunder roared again.

The night returned to darkness.

DeFeo turned, and started to run. Gabe tore after him.

"No, Gabe!" Morwenna shouted. "Let him go!"

Gabe looked at her briefly. "I can't," he said quietly.

He turned and ran after DeFeo. She saw Gabe catch hold of DeFeo again.

"Stay still—give in and stay still, please!" Gabe begged the other man.

It wasn't to be. DeFeo let out with a punch that landed hard on Gabe's jaw.

"No," DeFeo cried. "You have to win, and you know it. And I just have to escape you."

The man sounded almost gleeful.

Gabe twisted to secure the other man's arms, but DeFeo wasn't willing to give in. In the struggle, they began to roll. They rolled hard and fast, and she shrieked again in horror; they were rolling toward the ledge. She could barely see in the darkness of the night, but she could still hear the two and they kept rolling...

"Gabe!" she cried.

But she couldn't see the two men any longer; she couldn't hear them. There was no crunch of snow. There was no grunting, no sound of blows falling...nothing.

She felt Shayne behind her, setting his hands on her shoulders.

"Oh, my God!" she breathed. "We've got to find him."

"We'll go after him," Shayne promised. "We'll go after him. But we've got to work here first. And fast."

"Shayne—"

"Bobby is caught," Shayne said, and he looked into her eyes. "And...I'm sorry, Morwenna, so sorry, but if Gabe does lose...DeFeo could come back."

"Just get me out!" Bobby cried.

"Come on. Cindy—" Shayne began, spinning around.

Cindy was already waiting at the tree. "I don't even know what just happened. But we've got to get Bobby out from under there. And we're going to be all right. Come on!"

Morwenna looked at Shayne, and together they hurried to the tree. Shayne took the front position. Morwenna strained. Her muscles ached to the core. They strained and pulled, and slowly, with Shayne shouting instructions, they brought the snowmobile back to rest on its tracks.

She fell back in the snow, exhausted and amazed that Shayne's system had worked. Her brother walked to the snowmobile, hunkering down to help Bobby up. Bobby winced, trying to stand.

"Nothing broken," he said.

"The tavern is just up ahead. Take Cindy. Get her back to the tavern," Shayne said.

Bobby nodded, realizing that he couldn't help.

"Can you make it without the snowmobile?" he asked Bobby and Cindy.

"We will make it without the snowmobile," Bobby assured them. "You two need it."

Cindy nodded, hurrying to Bobby to lend support to help him limp along.

But, as Morwenna watched, Cindy paused, staring at Shayne with anguish in her eyes. She rushed to him, caught hold of his jacket, rose to her toes and kissed his lips.

And, if only quickly, Shayne kissed her back.

"We've all got to move!" he commanded.

Cindy nodded and ran back to Bobby.

Shayne mounted the snowmobile. The headlight

was still on; he turned the key in the ignition and nothing happened. He turned it again.

And the motor sprang back to life. Shayne carefully eased it into Reverse, and the mangled machinery moved.

"Go!" he said to Bobby and Cindy. He looked at Morwenna. "Climb on!" he told her.

She did so quickly, and they moved on into the darkness of the night.

Chapter 11

Bobby's leg was killing him. He was sure that he hadn't broken any bones, but he had done some mean damage to himself.

He leaned hard on Cindy for support, and they moved through the night. He could hear the strain of his breathing; even in the dim light of the moon that shone down upon them, he could see the massive mist of each breath he took.

Cindy labored at his side.

"I'm sorry!" he said.

"Oh, Bobby," she returned. "I'm all right, really. I'm tougher than I look, and I was never really hurt badly. I was frozen…blacked out a bit, but I'm all right. You can lean on me."

"Maybe you should run ahead," he suggested.

"Never," she told him. "Bobby, I don't understand anything about tonight."

"I'm not sure *we* even know what happened," he said.

"That light…" she murmured.

"Strange, huh?"

"Very!" she said. Then she stopped in her tracks. "Bobby!"

"What?"

"I can see it!"

"See what?"

"A star!"

"What?"

She laughed. "I see a star, and it's actually the tavern! The electricity must have just gone back on. Look! It's all lit up, and it seems like a zillion colors are shining out—oh, it's the lights on the tree, Bobby. I can see the tree with the star on top!

Look through the pines, and you can see the tree right through the window!"

He paused, and he peered through the trees.

And he smiled, unaware of the pain in his leg.

The star at the top of Mac's tavern tree seemed brilliant. It was a guide, and it was a sign.

They were almost there.

"Cindy, come on. Hot chocolate is so close I can almost taste it!"

They took the beat-up snowmobile around bend after bend.

And there was no sign of either Gabe Lange or Luke DeFeo.

Shayne drew to a stop, revving the motor as he tried to look around.

"Morwenna," he murmured. "We're not going to find them."

"No, no, no!" she said. "They've gone over the ledge. Oh, Shayne..."

"Maybe not, Morwenna. Gabe is a resourceful fellow."

"We can't give up! We can't give up."

"Morwenna, you can't go over the ledge. It's a far drop down."

"We can't give up."

"We have to. It's dark—the light isn't showing us much. They might be down over the ledge, but safe on some kind of outcrop. They might have wound up taking the fight up one of the slopes. They could have wound up in the trees anywhere."

He was right; she felt ill.

"Oh, Shayne!"

He turned and touched her cheek. "We could be heading for frostbite now, Morwenna. We have to go back. We need a helicopter, and we need light. We'll get Dad and Mac, we'll see if anyone has been able to get hold of someone who can really help," he said gently.

She nodded and leaned her head against his back. "Shayne, we tied him up!"

He nodded. "Yep."

"Genevieve never stopped believing in him."

"No," Shayne agreed. He cleared his throat.

"DeFeo arrived in a cop's uniform, Morwenna. We had no choice."

"But he saved Genevieve's life. And then...he might have saved all of us."

"He did save all of us," Shayne said.

She nodded against his back. Her heart ached. *This* hurt. This hurt in a way that was far worse than anything she had ever felt. It seemed silly and irrelevant that she had cared at all that Alex had been on a beach—chasing Double-D Debbie.

Shayne revved the motor and carefully turned the snowmobile.

When they finally reached the place where the fight had begun, Morwenna begged him to stop for a minute.

She crawled off the snowmobile and carefully moved toward the ledge.

"Wait! Be careful. I'll get a light."

She heard her brother swearing softly as he struggled to open the bent-up storage compartment on the side of the snowmobile that had hit the ground. She heard a wrenching sound as it gave, and then she was aware that Shayne followed her to where she stood with a high-powered flash-light.

Silently, they searched the terrain below them. The moon was casting a decent glow, and they looked and looked.

"Anything?" she whispered.

"No," he said.

"Try farther down, Shayne. Cast the light down."

He did.

But no one was there.

Shayne set his arm around her shoulders and led her back to the snowmobile. "It's good that we didn't find them, you know that, right?" Shayne asked her.

She imagined Gabe at the bottom of the moun-tain, crushed, mangled and bleeding.

"Yes," she said huskily. Silently, she crawled on the snowmobile behind him.

"Hey!" he said.

"Yeah?"

"The lights are back on at the tavern," he said.

"So they are."

★ ★ ★

Bobby wasn't sure he'd ever seen anything as beautiful as his mother's look of joy when he and Cindy stumbled into the tavern.

Ah, but maybe there was. It was Genevieve's face as she saw her mother.

"Mommy!" she cried. Delight in her voice. "Oh, Mommy!"

Genevieve threw herself against Cindy, who nearly fell over.

"Careful!" Connor cried. And then he was sobbing, too.

"I knew that Daddy would find you," Genevieve said. "I knew that he would!"

"I don't know how he even knew that I was out there!" Cindy said, accepting hugs from all around.

Bobby found himself crushed in a ferocious bear hug by his mother, and then his father. And he wondered if the way that his father looked at him with such pride and love wasn't one of the best gifts he'd ever received at Christmas.

Then his mother cried out, "Bobby, you're hurt!"

"Just a sore leg. My brother will fix it."

Stacy drew back, concern in her eyes again. "They're not here. Shayne and Morwenna. Where are they?"

Then he and Cindy tried to explain, each interrupting one another to add a detail.

"But—but they went to try to help Gabe. Against DeFeo!" his mother said, fear in her voice.

"They're on the snowmobile. They're fine. It's still working. And, Mom, honestly, I think that Gabe is going to rearrest DeFeo. I don't think there's any question," Bobby said.

Brian Williamson came over to them. "Bobby, get that wet coat off. Come on, everybody. These two need to be warmed up."

Mary jumped to at her husband's words, smiling as she hurried for her coat to put on Cindy until she could warm up. Bobby felt himself divested of his wet snow gear and bundled into an oversize coat.

"My God," Stacy said, hurrying to the window. "Where are they? Where are they?"

Cindy walked over to Stacy, touching her gently

on the shoulder. "Mom...I mean, Stacy, I'm so sorry. Shayne should never have been out. I don't know how he knew to come looking. I just can't believe that he did..."

Stacy turned to look at her. She reached out and drew her into a big hug.

"It's not your fault! It's not your fault at all for wanting to be with your family at Christmas. And you call me Mom forever, no matter what you two do in the future, do you hear me?" Stacy demanded.

Cindy nodded, tears in her eyes.

Mike walked up behind her, pulling her from his wife and into his arms.

"We are always happy to see you, Cindy," he told her. "Listen to your old dad."

Cindy started to cry.

Bobby felt tears welling in his own eyes.

"Now is the time for Irish coffee!" Mac boomed out. "Stacy MacDougal, come back here and help me. Those children need something warm in their bodies!"

"Yes, yes, of course," Stacy said. "And we'll need

to make two extra, because Shayne and Morwenna will be back any minute."

She walked around the bar to busy herself helping Mac.

The Williamson family stood near the window, watching, offering silent support.

Genevieve and Connor clung to their mother.

Bobby sat back in a booth, his leg up. His mother brought him the first steaming Irish coffee. He smiled at her. He sipped it. "They'll be here," he said firmly. He pointed at the star at the top of the Christmas tree. "It will lead them home, you'll see. The electricity miraculously came back on at the right time to see to it that the star leads them back. It brought Cindy and me in."

Stacy nodded. "Yes, yes, it did."

Bobby perked up suddenly. "Listen! Listen, I can hear the motor," he said.

"They're coming!" Adam Williamson said from the window. "They're coming!"

Stacy stood by Bobby, closing her eyes in gratitude. She looked at Bobby. "It's a beautiful sound right now."

★ ★ ★

Shayne slipped his arm around Morwenna as she crawled off the back of the snowmobile. She hadn't realized it, but her cheeks frozen on her face—and her "cheeks" were frozen elsewhere, as well. Without Shayne's arm around her, she might have stumbled.

The door to the tavern burst open.

Her mother and father came running out, heedless of the cold, hugging them both and urging them into the warmth.

Morwenna felt like a star, friends and family everywhere, helping her off with the wet and on with dry, a sweater and a scarf someone had once left behind, and held in the tavern's back room in hopes the owner would return for it. Her mother held her hands in her own, rubbing them and warming them. Hot, stiff coffee was set before her, and her father listened while Shayne explained where they had searched, and that they hadn't found anything.

She tried not to cry.

She couldn't believe that Gabe Lange had been

in their lives so briefly, and that she felt as bereft as she did. She wanted to pray that he was alive and was so afraid he couldn't possibly be.

She was vaguely aware of everyone talking as she sipped her laced coffee.

"DeFeo could still be out there," Mike said.

"You enjoy your family," Brian Williamson told him. "I've got the shotgun, and I'll be watching the front."

"And no one is coming in the back," Mac assured him. "Windows and doors are bolted."

"He's not coming back," Morwenna said. "Not unless...not unless Gabe is dead," she whispered.

"Gabe isn't dead!" Genevieve announced fiercely.

"Of course not," Morwenna said. She tried to smile at her niece. But Genevieve wasn't worried.

She was trying to reassure her aunt.

"Gabe isn't dead," she repeated. "He's going to find us all again." She pointed at the star. "He'll see it, too!"

"You're absolutely right," she told Genevieve. She wished she believed it.

She leaned back again, taking a long swallow of the coffee brew. It was good. The alcohol warmed her to the core. It seemed impossible, but she was warm again. She closed her eyes, and she listened to those around her.

She could hear Bobby and her father talking.

"I'm hoping for Juilliard, Dad," Bobby said. "I'm really hoping. And I will work my way through it. I wouldn't drop out, I swear."

"Son, not that I don't have faith in you—I do," Mike said. "But—here's the thing. If it isn't Juilliard, we'll search. We'll search until we find the right school. There's Ball State University of Music. There's Harvard. And, son, you will get into one of them," he said firmly.

"Thanks, Dad," Bobby said softly.

She opened one eye, and was glad to see them at the next booth, heads together, close.

She turned her head around a little, and there was Shayne.

With his family.

He was seated next to Cindy. They were close. The kids were on top of both of them; Shayne held his son in his lap while Cindy held her daughter. It was such a perfect picture.

She didn't know if they actually would get back together. But whether they did or not, they would always share a very special bond now, she thought. And the fighting would all be over.

She closed her eyes again. She smiled. It was good. And yet...

Her heart ached.

Morwenna looked at the TV to distract herself. The television was still snowy, but a picture was starting to show.

A newscaster stood on a roadway. Morwenna could see the buildings around her and she recognized the little town just at the base of the mountain. The reporter was standing just outside the police station.

"Police have recaptured escaped white-collar criminal Luke DeFeo," she said, her voice cheerful. "DeFeo managed to escape during a prisoner transfer yesterday, midday. It's Christmas for the cops, too! The con walked right into the police station, half-delirious, and gave himself up. One of the state's finest, Detective Gabriel Lange, had been in hot pursuit—we have no information as to Lange's whereabouts, but rescue crews are out now, searching for him. In other news, despite the snowstorm, electricity is being restored to about five thousand homes, and in all, it looks like a white and merry Christmas. Over to you, now, Walter!"

"How the heck did the man get down the mountain so fast?" Mac asked incredulously.

"Really, that's just about impossible," Mike said.

"You think they got the right man?" Bobby asked.

"Yeah, they flashed his picture up there in the corner, didn't you see it?" Mac asked.

"Maybe he fell down half of it," Stacy suggested.

"Well, they have him, and that's that," Bobby said. He limped over to Morwenna and slid into the booth next to her. "Gabe is going to be all right, too, then."

"Sounds odd, doesn't it, Bobby?" she asked.

"What's that?"

"DeFeo handed himself in," Morwenna said.

"He *handed himself in.* That really doesn't sound like the guy who was fighting Gabe on the mountain."

"But it was him, Morwenna. And," he said, offering her a smile, "they will find Gabe. And he'll be all right."

She smiled, squeezed his hand and leaned her head back again. She fingered the little angel on her chain.

But it was bitterly cold out. He was on a mountain. He could have fallen. He could be somewhere with his leg broken, or worse.

"Morwenna," Bobby said gently.

She opened her eyes.

"They have helicopters, they have search dogs, they know what they're doing," he said.

She nodded again.

Something seemed to flash before her eyes. She turned. The star on the top of the tavern tree seemed to be glowing more brightly.

Electrical surge! she thought.

"Bobby, let's see that leg. Mac will have something. You've got bruised muscles or torn ligaments, baby bro. I need to get you wrapped up," Shayne said, coming over to assist Bobby.

"Yes, sir," Bobby said.

He kissed his sister's forehead, and went to Shayne to have the damage assessed.

Genevieve came over to her. She looked at Morwenna solemnly. "Gabe is going to be okay. I know it, Auntie Wenna."

She put her arm around the little girl, pulling her closer.

"I'm sure he is. He was telling me a little story about the angels getting feisty at Christmas. And there's a fallen angel, you know."

"Lucifer," Connor said.

Morwenna smiled. Her nephew had come over to try to give her comfort, too.

"Right," Genevieve said. She was very grave. "Except that God loves everyone, even those who are bad."

"Fallen," Connor said, sighing with great patience.

Morwenna smiled. "When you get in trouble, you know your folks still love you, right?"

Genevieve nodded gravely.

Morwenna reached for one of the big white napkins in the holder at the end of the booth and found a pencil. She started to sketch for the children. "So, here, you see, here's Lucifer, who is like a bad child, trying to instigate trouble. Now, as you said, God loves everyone, no matter what, just like a parent loves a child, even when that child's behavior is not so good. But a parent knows when he or she has a kid who can cause trouble..." She paused, sketching an angel. "So he sends out a friend, or maybe even a sibling or a cousin, an angel who does behave, to try to make the mischief-making angel behave, and not hurt other people. Is that the story, Genevieve?"

"Yes!" Genevieve said. "Gabe was saying that God sometimes has to send out one of his good angels to make sure that trouble doesn't happen." She looked at her aunt in wonder.

"That's a nice thought, Genevieve," Morwenna said.

"It's a nice story! I really like that story!" Genevieve said. She touched the paper Morwenna had been drawing on. "You can draw in people," she said. "You and my dad and Uncle Bobby, Gram and Gramps, Connor and me. And maybe even my mom."

"Definitely, your mom, too," Morwenna agreed, and sketched.

When she finished, Genevieve reached up and touched the little gold angel that hung around Morwenna's neck. "We have angels," she said. "Good angels. Like Gram's little angel on her tree. I held it, and I dropped it, but I never broke it," she said.

"No," Morwenna assured her, hugging her again as she smiled at Connor. "You didn't break it— none of us broke what was really important today," she said. Looking over Genevieve's head, she noted the star on the tree again. It was odd how it seemed to be burning more and more brightly.

"As if it is leading someone home," she murmured.

"What?" Genevieve asked.

"Sweetie, let me get up," Morwenna said. Genevieve obliged, and Morwenna hurried toward the door, heedless of a coat or the cold.

The moon was out, and the glow from the tavern seemed to be lighting up the mountaintop as she burst out into the night. She saw nothing at first, and she felt the cold, and wondered if she was an idiot.

Then she heard a groan. She might have imagined it. But she hadn't.

She raced out into the snow, listening. "Gabe!" She cried his name, and ran along the edge of the trees. "Gabe!"

She heard something…a rustling. And then she saw the heap of a man in the snow.

She raced over to him, falling to her knees.

It was Gabe!

He lay as if he had been walking to the door, and then collapsed.

"Gabe! Gabe! Oh, my God, you're hurt, you're…" She touched his face, searched for a pulse.

His eyes opened, and he stared at her. He stared at her without a single sign of recognition.

"Gabe, it's Morwenna. You're hurt. We're going

to get you in. Oh, thank God, you're alive!" She couldn't help herself. She leaned in and kissed his lips, quickly. She moved away, just an inch, looking into his eyes.

She saw confusion…and yet, a strange sense of recognition. And she wasn't sure if she moved, or if he moved, but she found that she was kissing him again.

Or he was kissing her. And the kiss was good, and sweet, and natural. And if it weren't for the circumstances, she would want it to be much deeper, and far more…

Passionate.

But he had been hurt, and they were out in the snow, and others would be there. She broke away, touching his cheek tenderly. "I…" he began, but fell silent.

"It's all right. Don't try to talk. We're going to get you in, get you warm. Oh, Gabe!" she said. Tears stung her eyes. They were instantly like ice. She didn't care.

"I can't remember," he said. He winced. "My head…"

"May be a concussion," Morwenna said. "But it's all right. Shayne will know what to do. You're going to be all right. And I don't know how you did it, Gabe, but Luke DeFeo is in custody and—"

"DeFeo," he said. "Yes, I was chasing him and then…I don't remember."

"You were wonderful," she assured him, worried.

He almost smiled. He touched her cheek. "I know that I have been saved by an angel!" he told her.

She shook her head, clutching his hand. "No, *we* have!" she told him. She thought that she'd never really understand what had happened that Christmas on the mountain, and she couldn't help but wonder just what had been at play. Had she and her family been caught in a strange battle? A battle in which they had actually been given a choice between a fallen angel and a strange force for good that gave them back something special they had been missing as a family, and in life.

And now…

She smiled.

Was it possible? Had the angels taken on the flesh and blood of the men they had known in the last hours? And was the man she now faced in essence the same— but not the same at all?

She heard Shayne shouting to his father and Mac; her mother was out on the steps. They were all calling out with concern and joy that he'd been found. The church bells began to peal, and she remembered that it was still Christmas night, and the one service for the few people in the little mountaintop area would begin at eight.

It was still Christmas.

She stared down at Gabe, into the green of his eyes, and she realized that something about him was just a little bit different, and yet...

He was Gabe. And so much about him was going to be exactly like the man she had come to know.

Her family rushed around her. She was aware that her mother was scolding her for being out without a coat. Genevieve was hopping up and down, saying she had known that Gabe would come back to them.

Her father and Shayne got him to his feet. They started moving toward the tavern.

Morwenna followed, and paused, looking at the star on top of the Christmas tree through the tavern windows.

She smiled. "Thank you! Thank you so much!" she said, her voice a whisper in the night air. "And as Genevieve would say, happy birthday."

★ ★ ★ ★ ★